CW00821307

PRAISE

"An intriguing and haunting story about a woman, a man, and a decades-old mystery."
ALISON MOORE, AUTHOR OF *THE RETREAT*

"A spooky and impossible situation that steals up on you until you're questioning your own life choices."
ROZ MORRIS, AUTHOR OF *EVER REST*

"From its beguiling opening to its heart-stopping conclusion, *One Tuesday, Early* gently leads us into a world both familiar and nightmarish. Eerie, atmospheric and immediately gripping, there's as much delight to be found in what's held back as there is in what's revealed. Told in gorgeous prose, Lexi and Finn's story twists and confounds, always defying expectation, and always a joy to read."
CHARLIE CARROLL, AUTHOR OF *THE LIP*

ABOUT THE AUTHOR

Annalisa Crawford lives in Cornwall, UK, with a good supply of moorland and beaches to keep her inspired. She lives with her husband, and canine writing partner, Artoo. Her two sons have flown the nest, but still like a mention.

annalisacrawford.com

ONE

TUESDAY,

EARLY

ANNALISA CRAWFORD

www.vineleavespress.com

One Tuesday, Early
Copyright © 2024 Annalisa Crawford

All rights reserved.
Print Edition
ISBN: 978-3-98832-059-9
Published by Vine Leaves Press 2024

No parts of this publication may be reproduced, stored in a retrieval system, or transmitted in any form or by any means, electronic, mechanical, photocopying, recording, or otherwise, without the prior written permission of the copyright owner.

This book is sold subject to the condition that it shall not, by way of trade or otherwise, be lent, resold, hired out, or otherwise circulated without the publisher's prior consent in any form of binding or cover other than that in which it is published and without a similar condition including this condition being imposed on the subsequent purchaser. Under no circumstances may any part of this book be photocopied for resale.

This is a work of fiction. Any similarity between the characters and situations within its pages and places or persons, living or dead, is unintentional and coincidental.

Cover design by Jessica Bell
Interior design by Amie McCracken

For Peter, Connor & Ollie

CHAPTER ONE

LEXI

You're home. Standing in the hall with its lemon-colored walls and newly laid floorboards. The stairs are ahead of you, the front door behind, as if you've just walked through it. You're dressed for work—a slightly too tight tailored skirt and white blouse, hair neatly tied back—but you don't have your bag with you. If you were coming home, you'd have that.

Anyway, isn't it morning? Shouldn't you be *facing* the door? Shouldn't you be *leaving*? The keys are on the hook although you don't remember putting them there. You hold your hand up, mimicking the action of removing keys from the hook and returning them, trying to recall which action was most recent.

Your alarm clock is ringing out from the bedroom—so, definitely morning—but Finn isn't switching it off. It slices into the silence, which you hadn't noticed was silent until right now.

"Finn, I'm ..." Home? Back? Neither seems accurate but you can't pinpoint why. Does he know you were gone? Did you pop out quickly while he nodded off again?

Pop where? Where exactly have you been? You glance over your shoulder at the door to jolt the memory back into place. Because it matters that you don't remember.

"Finn—turn that bloody alarm off."

The clock at the foot of the stairs says 6:05 which means the alarm has been sounding for five minutes. Finn ought to be stomping around by now, bleary-eyed, complaining about how energetic you are first thing in the morning.

"Finn!"

You spring up the stairs two at a time, stopping abruptly at your bedroom door. He's not there. The bed is unused—duvet smooth upon the mattress, pillows uncreased. The beep-beep-beep of the alarm pierces your head until you crawl across the bed to switch it off.

The room is suddenly sterile, devoid. You feel a chill despite the current heatwave and overnight mugginess.

Across the landing, the bathroom is free of the steam and musky fragrances Finn usually leaves behind. The spare room is untouched, frosty from disuse. The study door's open—papers are scattered across the desk, Finn's briefcase thrown carelessly onto the floor as it always is after his tedious commute every evening.

Any second now, he'll appear at the top of the stairs and wonder why you're not getting ready for work.

"I'm dressed, aren't I?" you'll say defensively, although you haven't *got* dressed, have you, you just *are*. And isn't this yesterday's blouse?

Perhaps it's Saturday and you went out straight from work last night, returning now, drunk or stoned? It would explain the detached, fuzzy sensation—your head and body not quite in unison. It would explain the lapse of memory. It's been years since you partied to unconsciousness, though—you're not even sure you could make it past midnight, these days.

Anyway, the calendar on the wall of Finn's study says Tuesday. So yes, you should be getting ready for work, but somehow, it's not right.

The calendar also reminds you it's the longest day of the year, with its footnote in the corner of the square. Midsummer. The sun rose over an hour ago; daytime is fully fledged. Perhaps that's why you're so discombobulated. Around the country—at Stonehenge and Glastonbury—people have been gathering through the night to celebrate the solstice. You've always wanted to go, but Finn, grumpy and stoic, says it's a waste of time.

"You'd be squashed together with hundreds of strangers—hardly a spiritual awakening."

"That's not why I want ..." you say as he turns away with disinterest, so you shrug and let the rationale dangle in the air. Next year you'll go without him. Mila or Vanessa would jump at the idea of a few days away.

Inching along the landing, taking in everything which might be a clue or an anomaly, you return to the bedroom, your sanctuary. You sigh with pleasure when you walk into the room, ordinarily. Its pale green walls and cream furnishings are opulent and relaxing. Problems of the day dissolve when shoes are kicked off and toes stretch onto the carpet.

Not this morning, though. It's bereft of comfort, filled instead with ambiguity. If you concentrate, perhaps Finn will reappear—like that old magic trick where a marked card moves from the pack into a sealed envelope. A trick of the eye, a sleight of hand.

You slump onto the bed and lie star-fished, your head wedged into the crevice between the two sets of pillows. Your fingers seek the rigid edge of the mattress as you extend into the space Finn's left vacant.

You open your eyes. If it's Tuesday, the street should be waking up. The window's open, yet the usual sounds are absent. No purr of cars easing themselves out of driveways, or early dog-walkers heading towards the fields. Not even the woman who tap-taps along the pavement in stilettoes to catch the 6:22 bus.

Caught between one second and the next, you relish the serenity. But it's a fleeting sensation, deepening into unease. Where are all the people?

You roll off the bed and throw open the curtains, dazzled momentarily by the searing sunlight. The empty road is stark, like the opening of a dystopian film where everyone's been killed by plague or zombies.

"Don't be so stupid," you chide yourself, but it's weird, even so. Finn, you can almost understand—he must have gone into work early today and forgot to tell you. But the whole street missing, the neighbors who adhere to synchronized and habitual routines, all apparently taking the same day off?

You ring his mobile, but all you hear is a grating three-beep melody. You text: *Call me when you get this.*

Last night nags at you. Residual anger rises, simmering like water in a pan. The ghost of an argument hovers beside you. You're almost positive you went out, which is unusual for a Monday night. You recall sitting alone in a restaurant and pouring a drink, but it fades when you try to attach the details. No ... no, not alone—Finn was there. Or you were waiting for him and he arrived late. You had a second glass, possibly more. Such cool relief on a hot, irritating day.

You mooch. You open the door of the cupboard under the stairs—chock-full of shoes and winter coats and the vacuum cleaner with its multitude of attachments. You stand at the living room door and glance around for anything amiss. You're still searching for him.

Outside, the temperature is already rising. It's going to be another intolerable day if this is the heat that's begun it.

Finn's not here either. The long, straight back garden doesn't allow for hiding things. Uneven paving slabs lead to a gate at the end, which in turn leads onto an unkempt alley which runs the full length of your terrace of houses. The new vegetable patch is sprouting a furry growth of weeds, despite being freshly dug for seeds, despite the lack of rain. How do weeds thrive when meticulously cultivated plants succumb?

You open the rickety wood gate and peer through the narrow gap you create. You can't be too careful; anyone could be on the other side. You tense, ready to push the gate shut, or run, or scream. Whenever you're alone in the house after dark, you dread the shadows from house lights and swaying trees, convinced all sorts of monsters are waiting to pounce.

"Finn?"

You open the gate fully and look up and down the lane. Overgrown shrubs and brambles make it difficult to see very far. A school tie hangs in one of the trees; crunched up cans of cider are lined up on a wall.

The neighboring gate is ajar. Perhaps Finn heard a disturbance and rushed to help. They're in their late seventies—in this heat, people have been advised to check on elderly friends. People can die in hot weather. When Mr. Robinson leant over the fence on Sunday while you were breaking your back digging through impacted soil, his bald spot was red and blistered.

"No point doing that yet, love," he said with a chuckle. All you wanted to do was slap sunscreen on his scalp and force him into a hat.

You stood and wiped dirt across your forehead. "I bought seeds yesterday and I thought I'd get cracking. I've got a hose—I thought it would be enough."

"Nothing'll grow now, maid—it's far too hot. And you've got no shade in this garden, see." He tutted, but he was smiling affectionately. "What do they teach you kids at school these days?"

"I haven't been at school for a good while, Mr. Robinson."

"Tsh, you're a youngster! I'll lend you a couple of books, if you're interested. There's a bit more to it than you realize."

Their curtains are drawn, upstairs and down. Shadows from the tall hedge behind you dance on the glass, making it seem full of life. You knock on the back door.

"Hello?" You create a funnel with your hands to see through the kitchen window and press your ear to the glass. "Mrs. Robinson? Agnes? Can you hear me? Is everything okay?"

You want to do more, *ought* to. You try the door handle. Locked. Breaking in would be a step too far. What if they're away for a few days, or simply still asleep and you go barreling through their house and scare them to death? You can check back this evening, because right now you should be getting ready for work.

Work, right. You rush home, but the kitchen clock still says 6:05, and so does your phone. You switch on the radio which spits out fractured hissing sounds. You try other stations with the same result. Finn would suggest an overnight storm knocked out the signal, but it was a clear night, almost weatherless.

"Right," you say, trying to urge yourself into action. You wedge two slices of granary bread into the toaster and fill the kettle.

Still none of the usual morning sounds infiltrate the house. No tire-screeching paperboy as he skids his bike around corners; no sullen old lady picking litter from the pavement as she plods to the shop around the corner. No one leaving for work or arriving home after an exhausting nightshift.

The toast springs up with a metallic clatter, causing you to jolt then laugh at yourself. How ridiculous! You make coffee and butter the toast, spreading thick globs of marmalade over the top. The first bite sticks in your throat, and you leave the rest of it on the plate.

You meander into the living room and stand at the window, mug in hand. There should be a few kids, at least, scuffing along the road to school. There should be buses and cars. It should be later than all the clocks in the house are saying.

Finn hasn't replied.

In fact, your phone is as abnormally silent as everything else. You'd expect pinging notifications from Mila or Vanessa by now—silly comments or likes on your status updates from last night. Instead, 'page cannot be refreshed' is displayed on every app.

Agitation rises, a tight knot in your gut. You chew your fingernail. You tap your foot against the wall.

Finn hasn't even looked at your message.

You argued—perhaps he's punishing you by ignoring you. The reason for the argument is still obscured. There have been niggles, of course, for days, weeks. Silly upsets, annoyances rising to the surface. The heat doesn't help, everyone's a little more tetchy than usual. On and off over the past couple of months, you've considered leaving—you can't blame that on the heatwave. Is that what happened? You said you want to split up and he's the one who walked out?

No, of course not. Any second, he'll turn up, gasping for breath, waving a two-liter bottle of milk in the air.

"They ran out at the Spar," he'll say. "I had to go all the way down to the Premier." He'll pause and frown because you're sitting here forlornly. "What's wrong?"

"I couldn't find you," you'll say, and it already sounds pathetic.

"I was worried," you'll say, starting again, and it won't sound much better. "Can you give me a lift to work? The buses are being shit again."

If you wait.

Long enough.

CHAPTER TWO

FINN

The alarm goes off just after six, and Finn flings his arm across to hit the snooze button, eyes shut against the invasive sunlight. Lexi refuses black-out curtains; she prefers rising with the sun. During the winter, this means it's impossible to rouse her, and in summer she's up before the alarm, showered and dressed and drinking coffee by the time Finn crawls out.

He wakes angry—the residue of a dream loitering, the enduring exasperation of last night's bewildering and digressive argument. He wakes having barely slept, having dozed fitfully, having wandered the house restlessly. He wakes with apprehension, with the awareness of something not quite right.

He untangles himself from the duvet and stumbles into the shower, standing beneath the stream without moving, turning the temperature incrementally colder. His head is muddled, weighed down and exhausted. Even the fresh, sharp scent of shower gel has lost potency. He scrapes mud from his fingernails and scratches shampoo against his scalp. His hands sting in the suds, and he examines the blisters on his palms. Digging does that, he supposes, when you're not used to it. He dresses and wanders downstairs, straightening the knot of his tie and smoothing it against his shirt.

"Morning," he says, entering the kitchen, uncertain of the reception he'll receive. With Lexi, these squabbles are best glossed over. Given the amount she drank last night, she might not remember arguing at all.

He reaches for the mug which will be waiting for him on the table, an automatic action after years of the same daily routine—when Lexi hears the bathroom door, she makes herself a second mug of coffee and Finn his first. But his mug isn't there. Neither is Lexi. Normally, she'd be leaning against the sink, listening to the news while she finished her drink, or loading the dishwasher. If he's running late, this is the point she'd be calling up to him with her abundance of early morning dynamism.

Finn frowns, staring at the spot where she should be. The vacancy is unsettling. He turns on the radio to mitigate the silence. Turns it on because Lexi *hasn't*—her habit, her preference for noise. The closing trumpet of 'Absolute Beginners' fades and the newsreader runs down the headlines—all the usual predictable and boring nonsense.

He fills the kettle and rinses last night's mug. He ambles into the living room while the water boils, expecting Lexi to be groaning on the sofa, perhaps clutching a bucket, begging Finn to phone in sick for her and renouncing alcohol forever. Or scowling at him, her vexation unremitting. He opens the window to allow the breeze in. It's only slight, but the curtains flutter and the hairs on his arm prickle.

The recycling lorry creates a symphony of smashed glass and clanking metal. Behind it, the BMW driver from three doors down is revving his engine, trying to squeeze past. Finn smirks—he hates that jerk.

On his way back to the kitchen, he pauses at the foot of the stairs. A flash of movement catches his eye.

"Lex?"

He waits for a reply. The emptiness is unsettling, unusual—the pattern of the morning is disordered. It's almost seven o'clock, and he's going to be late.

He re-boils the kettle and makes a hideous sludge of instant coffee—there's no time for anything else. He gulps and grimaces, adding a spoonful of sugar which makes little difference. He grabs a handful of chocolate digestives from the biscuit barrel. Lexi usually has toast ready for him to swipe from the plate as he leaves.

"I'm off, Lexi," he calls. He glances back at the deserted kitchen, his foggy, fatigued head still trying to make sense of her absence. "See you later," he murmurs.

On the doorstep, he dances in and out of the house. Maybe he should stay home. Is it heartless to leave? He closes the door and walks to the car, then back to the house and pauses with his hand on the front door. People walking past cast curious glances. He smiles and nods, then jumps into the car. He drums his fingers on the steering wheel then drives away.

***

Finn's first proper coffee of the morning, from the shop near his office, is a relief—soothing his dull, throbbing headache.

It's busier than usual, people are everywhere: in the neat queue to place their order, in a cluster to pick up their coffees and croissants. They spill onto the pavement because the inside tables are all taken. In contrast with the normal pre-work crowd, these unfamiliar people are dressed in bright primary colors and carrying banners with slogans.

"They're protesters," says the barista clearing tables as Finn heads to the door. "There's something going on at the Plaza." She rolls her eyes.

Finn nods civilly, considering his response, but she's already moved to the next table and Finn is ejected into the fresh air, grateful for the breeze after the claustrophobia of the coffee shop. A ring of sweat sits along his hairline. It's going to be another scorcher, the forecast said.

The office is abuzz with the usual mundane chatter about last night's TV and what the kids did at school. Finn drops his bag beside his desk and switches on his computer. He waits with his head heavy in his hands while the machine whirs through its tedious start-up protocols. Eyes closed, he could easily fall asleep.

"Hey, Finn—ready for the nine o'clock meeting?" Rachel looms over him. He stifles a yawn and tries to focus. "Department meeting?"

"Right ... Sure." A tiny speck of a plane spearing though the spotless sky, glinting as it catches the sun and leaving a weakening vapor trail, distracts him. On the frenetic junction below, car horns beep and buses growl. A siren blares and vehicles scurry to the edges of the road. Finn winces at the sound.

"You okay? You look rough."

"Didn't sleep. Blasted heat."

"I thought we'd go to the conference room—it should be cooler in there."

There are six of them in the meeting. Rachel does the majority of the talking, working her way through a hastily jotted agenda. Recently promoted, she hopes she'll still be classed as *one of the team*, but of course she won't. She's their boss now. She's nervous about leading the meeting—there are awkward pauses while she searches for the correct document or asks a question no one wants to answer.

The protesters have congregated outside—on the Plaza right below this room. They're yelling about climate change, although the actual phrases are incomprehensible. Someone has a trumpet, playing a tuneless drone which elicits a roaring response from the crowd.

Rachel closes the window to block the noise, so now it's stifling. Finn glances at the clock—half-past nine. It's hard to concentrate with the temperature soaring, with his mouth dry and his shirt collar restrictive. His thoughts drift to Lexi, but he shoves her aside. His eyes droop, his interest in the meeting wilts. Rachel scribbles numbers on the whiteboard which Finn supposes would make sense if he'd been listening.

At ten, the meeting disbands and the six of them pour into the corridor the way Finn longs to pour cider into a glass. En masse, they go down to the small car park they share with the surrounding offices, grateful for the shade of the four-story buildings. They stand alone, lighting a cigarette or checking their phones, and the air revives them.

Eleven o'clock. Finn looks at the files piled on his desk— the paperwork he took to the meeting, swelled by the further amount he brought back. The incessant assault of his headache makes it hard to look at his screen for long, and the spreadsheet isn't giving him the answers he expected. He rummages his desk drawer for painkillers.

Twelve o'clock. One o'clock.

Finn calls Lexi out of habit. It goes to voicemail; he leaves the line open, recording dead air onto her messages. The automated voice tells him to hang up.

"Isn't she answering?"

"What?"

Rachel nods towards the phone in his hand. "Lexi. Isn't she answering?"

"Uh, no. How did you know ...?"

"You always call her at lunchtime."

"Not always."

"Or she calls you." Rachel raises her eyebrows. "Every. Single. Day. It's ... a bit weird."

Do they? When did *that* start? He shifts in his chair, embarrassed by the clinginess it implies. "Not *that* weird."

"Anyway, I'm going to grab some lunch. Do you want to come?"

"I'm not hungry."

Two o'clock. The afternoon's passing quickly. Three o'clock, four. Has Finn done *any* work today? He barely recalls. It seems only minutes since he arrived; the mess on his desk is as burdensome as it was this morning.

His phone remains mute. His messages are unread.

Five o'clock. Really? It can't be. Wasn't it four a moment ago? Finn leans back in his chair and watches his colleagues packing up for the evening. He turns off his computer and fumbles for his bag.

"Hope you manage to track down Lexi," Rachel calls with a wink. He pauses clumsily, waiting a beat too long to make a decent retort, and leaves.

An inordinate number of early evening idlers hinder Finn's march to his car. Once there, he crawls with the rest of the commuters, nudging along the dual carriageway, merging in turn with traffic from the slip roads. The cacophony of radio stations blasting through open windows causes his head to throb, reactivating the headache which was beginning to diminish. The sun dazzles him as he snakes around the bends and eventually crosses the bridge towards home. "I'm back," he announces, slamming the door and locking the day firmly on the other side.

Lexi doesn't answer. The post is on the doormat, yesterday's dishes are scattered across the kitchen counter, there's no aroma of tonight's dinner in the oven. The air is stagnant.

On a normal day, Lexi is home before Finn, finishing work at four and catching the bus almost immediately. On these recent hot days, he's found her sitting in the garden with a cider and a book, legs stretched out on the grass, or pulling weeds from the patch of earth she's claimed for growing vegetables. Today, she's neither inside nor out.

Finn changes into his shorts and splashes water on his face and neck. He grabs a beer from the fridge and snaps the tab. His exhaustion and niggling headache begin to disperse. He sits in the cool living room—the sun is at the back of the house in the evenings—and closes his eyes, allowing his body to become heavy and disconnected.

Seven o'clock, eight o'clock, nine. Finn phones for a pizza, leaves another voicemail for Lexi, and tries to enjoy the noiseless house. It doesn't happen often, that Lexi is out without him. He stands at the back door, leans against the jamb, and watches the setting sun. Cooler now, pleasant. Seagulls squawk from the rooftops. In the distance, the drone of traffic across the bridge floats on the clear air, and the evening train from London chunters through the fields.

Night falls without him realizing.

CHAPTER THREE

LEXI

It's 6:05 when you finish the coffee, shuddering at the bitter aftertaste, and stride to the front door. Just as it was 6:05 when you were making toast in the kitchen and 6:05 when you stood at the back gate whispering Finn's name. The hands of your watches are frozen—both the basic watch with its dull, scratched glass after years of wear, and the one fixed into a leather bracelet which makes it more jewelry than timepiece.

Normally, they tick in unison. Today, the minute and hour hands are fixed, while the second hands circle frantically, trying to settle into their rightful rhythm. You shake your wrist, attempting to incite them back into order.

The front door is locked, which is strange if you came in that way from wherever you've been. You unlock it and step out onto the drive. Finn's car is here. Is that a good or bad sign? If it's here, it's *not* with Finn—he wouldn't get far without it, so it must be a *good* thing?

"Come out, come out, wherever you are ..."

You trail your hand across the red paintwork, pausing at the front to press your palms flat against the bonnet. It's cold. Unused, unrequired for whatever scheme he's embarked on. Bobbing down, you peer underneath not sure what you expect to find there—certainly not Finn.

"What are you playing at?"

You sit on the low wall at the end of the garden, facing the deserted road. Your too-tight skirt rides up your thighs and creaks at the seams. Despite the clocks stalling, it must be 7:30 a.m., at least. You should be thinking about getting ready for the bus. What bus? None have passed so far.

And still no people. No teachers driving up to the school, no sign of the joggers who meet on the field to run their circuit together, no hum of traffic on the bridge that you can see from just along the road.

Sounds of breakfast time should be rolling out of the open windows. Kids being roused, the local radio station in stereo from at least three different neighbors. On this torpid air, you should hear the train to London thudding along the tracks. Seagulls should be squawking from rooftops.

And yet, nothing. You're alone.

You retreat to the house, scanning windows for someone peeking out and watching you, giving away the big joke they're playing on you. Your reflection in your own window makes you jump.

You lock the door. Then unlock it. In case Finn returns but doesn't have his keys on him. The silence swirls. You stand in the middle of the hall, helpless; you don't feel comfortable or safe in your own home.

"Finn, this isn't funny anymore."

There's no reply from him, no icon to say he's seen the message. No answer when you phone work to tell them you'll be late—you hang on the line until the relentless ringing drills into your head.

Now what? You could ignore this weirdness and read a book, watch a film. You could go back to bed and hope this is a bizarre dream you can escape from. You could.

But you don't.

Upstairs—one decision made—you unbutton your blouse and unzip your skirt, letting them fall to the floor, shedding them like a second skin. A skin you hate. The skin of a person you don't recognize when you wear them. Serious and professional, and nothing like you imagined your adult self would be. You unclip your hair and run your hands through it. You scoop the weekend's crumpled shorts and T-shirt from the floor; the pool of sunshine they've been residing in makes them hot against your skin.

It's a surrender, an acceptance of this absurdity.

And now? You could bake a cake, have another coffee, pull out Finn's weights from the spare room and have a workout in the garden. You could.

What would Finn do? He'd try to work out what was happening. He'd go searching for answers. He'd discount the implausibility he was alone because it's not logical. *It wouldn't happen, Lex, think about it!* He'd drag you along with him, to prove he's right.

Of course, he's right. But you'd resist like a petulant child. Nothing good can come from leaving the house. The front door is a sturdy barricade to the deserted road. Or perhaps, by now, not so deserted. Perhaps whatever delusion you're suffering has abated, and the world is happily plodding along while you're definitely going to be late for work.

Nothing good can come from staying here, either. The walls are constricting, and you can't quite catch your breath. Your uneasiness is increasing.

The resolute rush downstairs causes your hair to bounce, but once the front door is open, you're caught in the stillness again, the cloying heat taking your breath away. On the face of it, everything is normal. The roses in the Robinsons' flower bed are vibrant but beginning to wilt; the bungalow opposite is half-painted, turning from sage green to yellow; there's a film of sand blown on the wind from the Sahara covering the parked cars.

Well, go on then, says Finn in your head.

One foot in front of the other, down the drive, out onto the pavement, into the middle of the road.

See, you've got this.

Something moves in your peripheral vision. A shadow. You duck behind a car.

Even the quietest sound is a tsunami.

Meow.

A cat pads along the road without a care. A black cat with one white paw and a grey smudge on his nose. They're lucky, aren't they, black cats? If they cross your path. Or are they *unlucky*? You never remember which. This one leans against a lamppost and arches itself into an indulgent stretch.

It watches you as though *you're* the interloper, trying to decide if you're friend or foe.

Hand held out towards it, you crouch. "Hey kitty, kitty."

It slinks towards you, all four paws following a single line, resembling a catwalk model. Cat walk. Walking like a cat.

When it's close, but not too close, it sits and yawns. You eye each other warily. The cat stretches—front paws pacing forward while the back two remain rooted—and gracefully slides onto its stomach. You stroke its head, and it purrs.

"What's going on, eh? Any ideas? It can't just be the two of us left, can it?"

When your legs stiffen and you maneuver to sit, the cat flees and scurries into a thick holly bush in someone's garden. The leaves oscillate with the impact, and when they settle, you are heavy with sadness.

***

It's time. Time to leave, time to search for answers.

Despite the lack of movement, the houses don't appear abandoned. You picture people inside ducked down beneath their windows, ready to jump up and yell, "Surprise!"

Two doors' down, the front window is crammed with thirteenth birthday cards, the next along with condolences. Fragments of their lives displayed—their joys and their grief. You stand at the third window, peering inside with your hands held against the glass to shield it from the glare of the sun. Toys strewn on the floor, a mug on the table, a half-eaten slice of toast on a plate. As if someone's just this moment stepped out to the kitchen. You wait, but they don't return.

You step over miniature fences and ornamental hedges designating the boundaries of each property; you tiptoe through flowerbeds and trail your hand along brick and pebble-dashed walls. House after house after house.

The final garden has a water feature cascading melodically into a small pond. The trickle of water is a deluge of noise, growing ever more clamorous, almost painful, the way late-night TV becomes intrusive as you doze in front of it. You plunge your hand into the stream, unexpectedly cool. Fingers first, then wrists, forearms. The skin mottles purple; hairs stand on end with goosebumps.

Knock on the door, says Finn in your head.

"I can't. What would I say?"

Do it.

You do. You step forward, ring the bell, and jump back covering your mouth with both hands. Why? Why did you do that? There's movement, a noise perhaps, but nothing happens. Perhaps you just anticipated movement, expected it. You consider ringing again, but instead you walk backwards down the path, out onto the pavement again.

Surely this is what you *should* be doing—what Finn is trying to tell you to do. Banging on windows, yelling through letter-boxes, causing a ruckus.

You cross the road to the next terrace. Buoyed up, confident, determined. You knock on doors, ring bells, shout. Moving swiftly from one to the next; frantically, urgently. No one answers. Not one single person.

It's not possible. There has to be an explanation.

If you wait, they'll reappear. They'll be furious at you for staring through their window, or waking the baby, or disturbing their shower. You'll have to run away, praying they don't recognize you. You'll run all the way home and Finn will ask where the hell you've been.

At the end of the row, when the adrenaline wanes, the stillness is crushing.

"There's got to be someone."

You clench your fists.

"Answer the door."

"There's got to be someone here. Answer the fucking door."
You stoop to pick up a small ceramic frog—it's cartoonish face mocks you with a wide smile. And you throw it. Such a quick, spontaneous action. Perhaps you meant to smash it onto the path, but it hits the window and the glass cracks. The aroma of bacon fills the air, and a blast of the local news on TV. A bus passes behind you but vanishes when you turn.

Everything silent. Everything stopped.

"Hello?"

Backing away from the house, you stand in the middle of the road and spin slowly around, taking in every shadow and reflection. Around and around.

"I know you're here. I heard you." Louder, slightly more animated. "Hello!"

Standing in the road and hollering into the air, making a kerfuffle.

"Answer me!" Around and around, faster. The houses and trees and searing blue sky whizz and whirl past, blurring into a streak of color.

The sound reverberates around the houses and down the small gaps between them, and across the road and back again.

And no one comes. No one hears you.

"Helllooo ..." Desperate, frantic.

Your voice snags on the air as if it's barbed wire. Your tangled *hello* goes on and on. You follow it along the road until your legs forget how to hold you up and you land heavily on the tarmac. Tears stream down your face. You catch your breath in big, painful clumps.

CHAPTER FOUR

FINN

Finn wakes just after six, despite disabling Lexi's alarm because Lexi's not here.

"Bloody woman," he mutters. Her early mornings have scorched themselves upon him without him realizing. He considers the other ways she might be modifying him. Fewer trips to the pub, more to the DIY stores; updating his wardrobe, one sloganed T-shirt at a time; less meat on his plate and additional salad.

The duvet lies heavily across him, too bulky for this weather. He kicks his legs out from beneath it and thrusts it onto Lexi's side. *She's* the one who craves the comfort of it, coiling herself into a ball despite the temperature. He'd be happy with a light cotton sheet.

The house has a different atmosphere this morning—he endures the emptiness now he knows to expect it. He has a shower, but takes his time, uncertain whether he should go to work or wait to see if Lexi will appear. Is it wrong to pretend nothing's wrong?

In the kitchen, he makes his own filtered coffee and toast. He sits at the table to eat, but Lexi's vacant chair opposite discomfits him. Maybe he doesn't need to remain at home, after all—what good would it do? It won't bring her back any quicker. He runs upstairs to change and goes to work.

The coffee shop is quiet without yesterday's protesters. Finn buys coffee and walks to the office on autopilot. When Rachel spots him, she enquires after his *missing girlfriend* with a playful smile.

"What did you say?"

She falters at his abruptness. "I just ... Yesterday, remember? She wasn't answering your messages ..." Her hands swirl in the air. "It was a joke."

"It wasn't funny."

She purses her lips. "Apparently not."

"Rach, wait."

She turns but he doesn't know what to say next; he doesn't want to say the thing he'll have to admit at some point, that Lexi's gone. His silence and her indifference force them into the opposite corners of the room.

Finn slumps into his chair and opens his email. The screen is filled with people wanting things from him—urgent requests highlighted in bright red, demands for information which could be sought elsewhere, long chains which have buried their original point. None of it important. His head is foggy. He turns his chair to the window and watches the clouds drift past.

Every so often, he checks his phone for messages or missed calls.

***

The following day, being alone in the house is unsettling. Each time he walks into a room, he expects Lexi to be there, looking up from her book with a smile, or poking her head into his study to ask if he wants another coffee. Shadows at night seem to fold into the shape of her, dancing on the walls as car head-lights flash into the room on their way past.

By Friday, the house is hostile, closing in on him until he fills every room with no space for anything else. Noises and creaks which usually go unnoticed are becoming louder. The hum of the fridge is grating, the ticking clock in the hall, irritating. He swears he hears her whispering his name.

He grabs his keys from the hook and is half-way to the door when the landline rings. He pauses, considering ignoring it, then thinking better of it. What if ...?

"Lexi?"

"No, it's Phoebe. Is Lexi not there?"

"Oh, um, hi. No, she's not."

"Oh. But it's Friday. We always talk on Fridays."

Perhaps he should have called her, prepared her for the idea of a missing niece. After all, she's Lexi's only family—her and Finn himself. "I know."

"Is everything okay?"

He takes a breath, a pause, a moment to decide. "She's gone." The words are wrong, untested. But it's been three days, what else can he say?

"What do you mean, gone?"

"We had an argument," he says quietly.

"What about?"

"Nothing important. This and that. She had a couple of drinks and it escalated."

"Important enough for her to disappear. Has she left you, properly *gone?*"

Properly gone. Left. Not coming back. A five-year relationship simply evaporated as if it meant nothing at all.

He stands in the middle of the living room, staring at the shelves full of her things, noting briefly that *his things* have been consigned to the study, like a teenager's belongings confined to one room.

"I don't know."

"Has she taken her clothes?"

He grunts.

"Have you phoned her at work?"

"No, I didn't think—"

"Has she been using her bank account?"

"How would I know? It's not like I keep tabs on everything she does."

"Finn, focus. This is important." She's becoming frustrated, concerned. "She would tell me if she'd left you, she'd have phoned me or even asked to stay here." She breathes heavily down the line. "She could be lying in a ditch, and we'd have no idea."

He pictures Lexi, eyes unblinking, lying in a dark, damp ditch and shudders. "All I know is she isn't here."

He's in the hall now. The calendar on the wall is scrawled in Lexi's handwriting—chores and errands are ticked off as she's done them, evenings out with friends are smiley-faced. He traces the letters of DENTIST!

"Have her friends heard anything?"

Phoebe's shrill voice echoes up the stairs and onto the landing. She was head mistress of a primary school before she took early retirement last year. Finn imagines her looming over her pupils, berating them for small indiscretions, the way she's doing to Finn now. *Focus.* Do they still sit cross-legged on the floor, staring up at their intimidating teacher? She hasn't lost her firmness. He thinks she must have been quite imposing to a seven-year-old.

"I don't know," he says weakly.

After Phoebe hangs up, after he's spent several minutes consoling her, Finn heads to the pub. He can't be in the house a moment longer; he can't handle Phoebe's clipped, imperious tones replaying in his head. Several blokes are hanging around the entrance, smoke billowing above them. The beer garden is teeming with parents and kids playing on the plastic tree-shaped slide while cold chips congeal in ketchup on their plates. He flinches at their glee-filled shrieks and sidesteps into the bar—dark, cool, sparse.

Familiar faces are already inside, a rumble of banal chit-chat wafting around. No one he knows by name: the guy with the Doberman that usually gets a sausage roll treat from the landlord, the father and son who sit side-by-side and stare resolutely ahead, making random comments about whichever sport is playing on the TV above the bar. A mismatched couple sit in the corner—he's wearing ripped jeans while she's dressed to the nines, reveling in admiring glances from the barman. Lexi has to be smart for work, so at the weekend she prefers jeans and T-shirts. She wears make-up sparingly, less than she used to.

He's two pints in when Dean arrives and automatically orders him another, despite the half-full glass in Finn's hand. "Got a pass from Lexi then?"

Finn's expression hardens. "She's gone." It isn't any easier to say it a second time. He feels sick as the words take shape.

"Properly gone? Packed her bags and ...?" Dean makes his fingers walk across the beer-sticky table.

Properly gone—the same phrase Phoebe used. Instead of what, pretending? Hiding in the shed until he's forgotten her, then jumping out and yelling "Surprise"?

Finn shrugs. "I guess."

"Oh, mate, I'm sorry. I didn't realize things were ... like that."

"Yeah, well." He presses the glass to his lips without drinking. He glances at the door as new people arrive, noisier people who glance around with embarrassed giggles and demur to the low-key ambiance.

Dean swigs his pint. "Had a bird do that to me once. Took all her stuff while I was at work one day. Took most of mine, too, to be honest." He laughs, forced, incredulous.

Finn wonders how long it took to move past the anger, to make it an anecdotal aside.

"You want another one?"

"Girlfriend?" Finn asks dryly.

"Well, if you're joking about it already, perhaps it wasn't such a bad thing."

"It's my round."

***

It's late when Finn gets home, past midnight—not *late*, but Lexi-late. If she were here, she'd be huffing in bed, eyes shut, pretending to be asleep. If she'd been at the pub with him, they'd have been home an hour ago.

He trips over Lexi's trainers—kicked off and discarded the last time she came back from a run—as he stumbles through the door and his ankle twists awkwardly.

"At least you could have taken these with you!" He grabs the shoes and hurls them into the garden. One bounces across the road, the other flies over next door's fence.

He sees her jacket. And her sunglasses. In the living room, her books on the shelves. Her ornaments and CDs and the stupid snow globe from Berlin. *Her* stuff everywhere, cluttering every surface. He swipes his hand across one of the shelves and everything crashes to the floor. He scowls at the mess and rummages the kitchen drawers for a black bin liner.

"So much crap, how much does she need?"

He fills the bag, all her things thrust inside, until it's too heavy to lift. He gets another. And another. Upstairs, he shoves her clothes inside, the hangers too, so they slice the bag open, and the contents spill out.

And, oh how his rage expands and engulfs him until he's exhausted and dizzy from the exertion and the plentiful lager and the sweltering mugginess of the night.

In the bathroom, he chucks her toiletries into the bath—the gels and liquids and creams. Why does she need so much! Glass bottles shatter, plastic ones split, and the contents mingle in a haze of lurid color. He opens a pot of body butter and smears it across the tiled wall.

He cries. Not the grief-stricken sobs of someone left behind, but the emotional explosion of a toddler unable to control his energy. He crawls into the bedroom and lies among the piles of Lexi's clothes. He pulls her T-shirts and skirts towards him in a bundle, curling himself around them and inhaling her scent.

The floor becomes uncomfortable after a while, but he sleeps deeply, and the next day his muscles are stiff and his bones ache. His throat is scratchy and swollen. He takes a moment to orientate himself. Head spinning, he sits up and notes the mess around him.

"What the ...?"

He staggers to the bathroom, peeing with his eyes half-closed against the sun reflecting off the badly positioned wall cabinet. He drinks from the tap, lapping water like a cat, and gazes into the bath. Pink and brown and green liquids leech into each other. What the hell happened last night? Downstairs, the chaos is worse. Chairs tipped over, a leg snapped in half. Books scattered with their pages creased and spines cracked. Plates and mugs smashed on the floor; several tiles chipped. Has he been burgled? He runs through his patchy recollection but nothing useful appears. The throbbing increases.

He checks the door, and although the front is unlocked, it doesn't appear anyone but him has been in the house. The TV and games console are untouched. His wallet is where he left it on the table.

"Shit."

He switches the kettle on and vomits in the sink.

CHAPTER FIVE

LEXI

Everything's clearer after rain. The horizon becomes a sharp edge sliced into the vibrant sky; small details are carved into it. Dust in the atmosphere is dampened while the petrichor rises. The smell of the woods where you built dens with Mila and swung across the small stream on a rope, and the first cut of grass in the spring.

But it hasn't rained for days. A haze sits around town and the air is fuzzy and distorted. You want to throw off the heat the way you'd discard a duvet.

Each step now is uncharted—moving further away from the house, from Finn, from all certainty. You're exam-day nervous. You're job-interview terrified. With every turn down a different street, you expect to bump into someone you know, to laugh with relief and describe your morning. You like groups, crowds; the camaraderie of commuters flowing in the same direction; or watching the Next Big Thing on TV, knowing millions of others are too; or watching fireworks on Bonfire Night because everyone is following the same tradition.

You skip to distract yourself. You jump on the cracks between paving slabs; you balance on the curb, arms out-stretched, deep in concentration. The road is lined with Victorian terraces; their dark, vacant windows with intimidating shadows observe your progress. You're almost at the high street without realizing this is where you were heading.

At the top of the road, you duck through the gates of the park—a triangle oasis of lawns and flowerbeds and two-hundred-year-old trees. You listen for birds that ought to be cawing and twittering from the branches. You hold your palm against the coarse bark of the enormous Scots Pine and imagine the people who've sheltered from the rain beneath its great span, or leant against it for furtive kisses, or climbed it after drunken evenings on the Waterside.

How many times you've passed this park on the bus, on the way home from work, or laden with shopping and too busy to just sit for a moment. Think of all the things you've missed, simply by scurrying through the day, ticking off lists that really don't matter. When you get back, you'll live differently, you'll make time, you promise yourself.

When?

If?

You close your eyes and take a breath and refuse to think anymore.

Leaving the park from the tip of its triangle, Fore Street stretches out in front of you—down the hill towards the two bridges leading out of town. Jammed with traffic, usually, with people flowing in and out of the shops, sitting at tables outside the cafes, greeting people, chatting, passing time. This is where you thought they'd be, the ones like you, left behind. Assumed. Hoped. This is where they *should* be. But they're not. This road is as bereft as the others.

As you wander, your reflection slinks alongside you in the shop windows. The more you see yourself, the larger and more distorted the panes are, the more remote you appear, until you're not even sure the reflection is you. In the middle of the empty street, you give in, you sit on the edge of the curb and feel all momentum drain from you.

A wave of heat, like a reassuring maternal hand, presses down until you're lying flat on your back staring up at the infinite sky. Directly above, there's none of the haziness which is fraying the edges of town—it's clear and bright. Not a dot of a bird, or the feather of a cloud.

You could fall asleep easily right now. And when you wake, Finn will be lying beside you, and it'll be dark—long before the alarm is due to go off. He might be propped up on his forearm, shaking you awake because you called out in fright and woke him.

You might be screaming right now.

He'll be annoyed, or he'll draw you towards him in a reassuring embrace which may escalate into unanticipated desire—it's difficult, these days, to tell how he'd react. You've been on edge with each other for weeks, tiptoeing around the problems.

Either way, when he wakes you, you'll be baffled, unsure where you are, convinced by the veracity of the nightmare you've just escaped.

You sit, awaiting being woken, and fold your knees into your chest. The scene ahead looks like a photo, a moment between moments. The earliest photographs of busy roads often looked empty because the exposure time was so long—in reality, they were all dipping in and out of shops, promenading arm-in-arm, unaware of the man with the black box. They were out of step with the camera. Is that what you are, trapped in the shutter of a camera?

Or, maybe, trapped somewhere else, trapped between ...?
No. Not that. Not yet. You won't allow *that* thought in your head. Too soon. Too terrible to comprehend.

What now? Sit here, wait?
That's not exactly a plan, is it? Finn mocks you with words that are yours, with a tone of voice you're imposing on him.
"Oh, piss off."
You've been saying that a lot recently. When did it start? When did the love and fun turn into boredom and resentment? It's been a smooth slide from the wave of adoration you felt when you met to the irritation which niggles at you now. Nine years older than you, Finn had his life sorted while you were still growing and developing. Your passing whims and great plans were alien to him, so he tempered you and you didn't notice at first. Gradually, his fierce, passionate embraces have turned into a chain of thorns snagging at your dress.

Yet, when you imagine life without him—when you have no idea where he is—you're exposed and fearful. He's in your every pore, as essential as water or air or the sound of people around you.

You take your phone from your back pocket and text Mila: *I'm having such a bizarre morning. I need to talk to you.*

No reply, of course. If people are missing, if Finn and your neighbors are gone, Mila and Vanessa and Cassie will be too.

Phoebe! Your aunt suddenly pops into your head—why wasn't she one of your first thoughts? Surely, *she's* safe. Across the river, five miles due east, pragmatic and resourceful Phoebe wouldn't put up with this nonsense. You tap her name from the list of favorites. Little dots dance across the screen, but the call doesn't connect. You didn't really expect it to.

All your friends and family and colleagues and ex-colleagues and ex-boyfriends, who may or may not exist anymore, swamp you—a cascade of all the people you've ever known all the people who've meant something special, or those who appeared in your life for fleeting but significant moments. How did you forget them?

It's too much. There are too many people to feel responsible for, to have an instilled obligation to. Why you and not them? Why did you get trapped in this red-hot nightmare? Concentrate. Think. Perhaps it's not them who left. Think back.

"NO!"

Once more, you're running. Mila's house is closest. She'll be there, and she'll make this all right. A breakdown, a crisis. She'll get help. She'll know what to do.

Mila's house is silent, the semi-circle of houses either side are too. You ring the bell, and bang on the door, and shout through the letterbox.

"Mila, Mila, open up. Please, I need you." Your voice reverberates along the hall.

She'll be in the kitchen, yelling for one or other of her kids to come and fetch their lunch or their homework. She'll be repeating all the stuff she needs to remember: wallet, wallet, wallet, text Lexi, text Lexi. She'll be in the hall with book bags and PE kits, scurrying to open the door at the sound of your panic.

And everything will be okay again, because she'll be there, and she'll take care of you.

Scurry, scurry, open.

The door remains shut. Locked.

"Mila?" You press your ear to the glass. With two kids, her house is usually a flurry of turmoil. "Please." You slide to the ground, sit on the step, and rest back against the door.

So often, you've sat here with a mug or glass in your hand, gazing across the valley to the secondary school rising high on top of the hill near your house. Except, today, not everything is visible. The school is veiled; the tops of the trees beyond it are missing.

The haze in the air is not a haze after all, but a mist dancing over the fringes of town.

It starts small.

You barely notice.

No more than a bubble, a tiny quivering speck.

You hold your breath to keep it inside. It dances and bounces, punches low in your gut and up into your throat.

It's a ball and a fist and a whimper and a yell. All swallowed down and shackled within you.

You want to run again, but your legs are immobile, frozen.

The morning replays itself in your head. Glimmers of stolen people flash before you.

Alone.

Breathing erratic and quickening. Breathing but struggling. Lungs seared with hot air. Breathing yet suffocating.

Gasping, groping for oxygen.

The world swirling and rushing towards you. Disembodied sounds thundering and falling. *Your* sound. *Your* cries. They fill your head; they explode inside you.

The fear. The terror.

Alone.

You curl into a ball and remain there for minutes, days, years, no time at all. You weep. You rock to the rhythm of your heartbeat. At some point, you'll unfurl and move on, because that's all you have left.

CHAPTER SIX

FINN

By Sunday afternoon, the drunken destruction wreaked on Friday night is bagged and ready for the bin men. A few broken tiles and a missing chair at the dining table are the only signs of anything amiss, when actually *everything* is amiss. Everything Finn thought he knew about Lexi and their relationship, has been blown into a million pieces.

Five days without her. Five days of expecting her to come through the door and kiss him as if nothing had happened. He opens the windows in every room, airing the house and his head. He stands at the front room window and gazes along the road. People pass by and catch his eye. He turns away.

The heatwave crashes to a theatrical conclusion with sheet lightning flashing across the late afternoon sky, followed by a long, low rumble of thunder. Kids playing outside shriek in mock terror. When the rain comes, Finn watches them getting drenched with a smirk. Rain so heavy it bounces off the pavement and off the grass because the soil is compacted and parched. It courses along the edges of the roads and gushes over the drains.

It lasts most of the evening, the thunder becomes a single, constant rumble in the background. The cooling temperature is a relief. Finn stands out in the garden and lets the rain soak him. He imagines Lexi mesmerized beside him.

He's been dozing on the sofa rather than going up to bed, barely settling into a full night's sleep anyway. Lexi always goes up before him, and he's used to sliding in beside her and wrapping his arms around her. A few times a week, she's naked beneath the duvet, inviting him to let his lips roam her body. The bed is unfamiliar without her.

***

It's Tuesday. Tuesday again. A whole week since Lexi went and his world tumbled down. He pounces on every phone call expectantly, every knock at the door with gusto. But it's never her.

When the phone rings this evening, it's Phoebe. "Is she back?"

"No. I would have told you."

"I think it's time to call the police." Her voice quivers.

He frowns as he tries to form the right words. "She's gone. She's not—"

"If you don't, I will. This isn't right. Lexi wouldn't leave without saying something. I know she's in trouble."

Finn sits heavily. This is real. It's not a dream or misunderstanding. "Okay. I'll do it. It should be me."

He waits a while before phoning. He rehearses what he's going to say. He makes a coffee and gazes at the back garden. Weeds are springing up in Lexi's fledgling vegetable patch, nourished by the rain. It doesn't take long for things to move on, does it?

Imagining Phoebe tapping him on the shoulder, he dials and waits.

The house contracts around him, the walls squeeze him. He wants to throw the phone to the floor and run outside. He lies on the living room rug, staring at the streak-marked ceiling where the paint didn't quite cover. Lexi went on about it for weeks before forgetting about it and moving on to a new grievance. Always one thing or another.

"... how can I help?"

Finn sits abruptly. "Hello? Yes, I'd like to ..." He'd like to hang up. He'd like to pretend everything's normal. "My girlfriend's missing." He closes his eyes at the word *missing*. It still doesn't feel right. He exhales slowly.

A torrent of questions follows: her name, date of birth, his name, any reason he can think of why she might have left, the date she left, her state of mind.

"Do you have any reason to suspect Lexi might be in danger?"

Finn puts the phone on speaker and sets it on the floor beside him, letting the voice on the other end roll around the room. *Missing. Danger.* These aren't words people use every day. This is not *every day*. He runs his hands through his hair.

"I'm not sure." Define *danger*.

"You've waited quite a while to report Lexi missing, sir?"

"Yes," is all he says, but it's probably the wrong thing.

"Well, Mr. Carmichael. I think I've got everything I need for today. If I could arrange a time for an officer to come round to get a few more details ..."

***

Finn digs holes in Lexi's vegetable patch for the seeds Lexi bought but never planted—carrots, beetroot, peas—following the instructions on the packet carefully. It seemed a shame to let them go to waste. With her trowel—a lilac one from a set she was given one Christmas—he widens the trench and places the seeds within, spacing them attentively. He fills the holes and presses the earth firmly, leaving fingerprints in the mud.

It's something to pass the time while he waits for the police to arrive, something to distract him. He had to take the afternoon off work, letting Rachel know in muted tones the reason for his absence, ignoring the look of surprise and concern on her face. It was a relief to have a reason to leave—everything about his job and the office seems trivial now.

Pottering in the garden is remarkably relaxing, even when that old git next door leans over the wall to interfere. Maybe Lexi was on to something after all.

He's out there when the doorbell rings. He wipes muddy hands across the rear of his jeans and opens the door to PC Rosevear who is every bit as tall and solid as Finn himself. Intimidatingly so. Both of them in the middle of the hall barely leaves space to maneuver. Finn leads him into the kitchen, and they sit at the table.

The constable recaps the information Finn gave over the phone, pausing every so often to clarify or expand on some point or other. Testing me, Finn thinks, trying to catch me out. He nods, mostly.

"Has Lexi taken her passport? Bank cards?"

"I'm not sure where she keeps her passport." He casts an eye around the room, as though it might magically appear. "Her bag's not here. Her cards are usually in that. In her purse."

Finn leads PC Rosevear around the house, watching as he opens the wardrobe—Lexi's side empty after Finn's dimly-remembered drunken rampage—and her drawers. The dressing table is equally sparse. The officer moves the few remaining items around like chess pieces and runs a finger across the surface to assess the dust.

He peeks into the spare room and the study, scanning Finn's desk. "May I?"

"It's my room, really. Lexi rarely comes in here." Finn indicates the bookshelf with a brief nod. "Those books are hers, though."

"I believe you argued before Miss Peters went missing?"

"Just a silly spat, nothing important."

"Do you argue often?"

"No more than anyone else, I imagine." He shrugs. How does one relationship stack up against another? How is one better than the next? Is there a point system: two arguments a month and you slide down the rankings?

The constable smiles reassuringly. "We all argue occasionally, Mr. Carmichael. Has Lexi mentioned anything out of the usual recently? Being followed, a new acquaintance, strange phone calls—anything which made her feel uncomfortable?"

"No, nothing like that."

They make their way back to the kitchen. "I'll need a list of Lexi's friends, colleagues at work, anyone you can think of she sees regularly. You've been gardening." He points to the vegetable plot, to the watering can and muddy footprints on the path.

"I thought I'd give it a try."

"Can I take a quick look?" He opens the door before Finn can reply. Finn remains in the house, watching as PC Rosevear walks slowly down the garden, inspecting the ground. He pushes the toe of his boot into the damp soil and returns to the house. He wipes his feet on the doormat. "Well, I think we've covered everything, sir." He glances down at his notepad and taps his pen against it. "Is there anything you'd like to add to your statement? Anything else you've thought of which might be relevant?"

Finn shakes his head and stares into the garden.

"Okay. Well, thank you for your time. We'll be in touch. I'll see myself out."

***

Finn calls in sick the following day. Indeed, he's felt sick ever since the police officer left. There was something unsettling about having a stranger scrutinize him with that air of smooth skepticism.

He keeps the curtains shut at the front of the house, hiding there, waiting for something but not knowing what.

A knock on the door cuts into his silence; the bell ringing follows quickly. Lexi's friend Vanessa is the only person Finn knows who's that impatient.

"What the hell is going on?" Hands on her hips, eyes flashing. "I've just had the police round mine asking questions about Lexi. She's missing and you didn't think to tell me! You didn't think to warn me they'd be coming. What the fuck is wrong with you?"

He stares blankly. The contrast of the dark front room and the glare of the sun out here throws him. "I'm sorry. I ..." He runs his hands through his hair and falters.

"Well, what happened? When did you last see her?"

"Last week. Tuesday."

Her mouth forms into a little O which curls into a smirk. "Has she left you? Is this a ploy to gain sympathy?"

"You think I'd waste police time like that? Piss off. I know you've never liked me, but that's low, even for you."

"You're full of shit."

"As you like to tell Lexi constantly."

Vanessa peers past him into the house, beady eyes darting left and right.

"Anyway, it's taken you over a week to figure out she's not around. How come? Perhaps you know exactly where she is, and she's sent you to spy on me. Is that it?"

"Don't be absurd." But she bristles and her nose twitches. "I'll be back. If I don't hear from her, I'll be back."

"I look forward to it."

She opens her mouth to say something more, then scowls and shakes her head. She turns on her heel and storms back down the drive. He skulks back into the shadows of the house.

The following day, the story of Lexi's disappearance is in the local paper—a half-column article asking for anyone with any information to get in touch. Finn wonders what little gems Vanessa's shared about him. The day after that, Lexi's on the regional news—her photo on their forty-inch screen makes her larger than life-size. He switches it off. He can't bear to see that photo one more time.

***

A second week passes, and a third. More and more Tuesdays crossed off on Lexi's calendar. Instead of sitting at home, he goes to the pub and watches sport he has no interest in. Dean sits with him for a couple of pints, sometimes, but bows out when his wife texts asking what time he'll be back. It makes no difference to Finn; their conversation is skeletal and functional.

He doesn't sleep. He lies poker-straight, staring at the ceiling. Even though he's made it back into the bed, he doesn't face Lexi's side—he's scared he might catch a glimpse of her. Occasionally, his arms spread out in search of her, and he flinches when they reach the cold, vacated space.

In the mornings, he stands at the open front door, suit on, keys poised. But the neighbors are watching and it's getting harder to get into the car, harder to navigate the daily rush hour. He's stopped going to the coffee shop, preferring to race directly to his desk. Rachel invites him to lunch, which she often does, or for a drink after work which she's never done before. He declines both.

He's trapped in the uncertainty. People are talking about him. They eye him suspiciously when he walks past. He's not sure if he's allowed to laugh or enjoy a film or sit with a pint and the rugby while his girlfriend is missing. He's not sure if his whole existence should be focused on Lexi. How long should it last? What if—?

He starts to arrive late for work or leaves early.

He phones in sick with barely a word of excuse.

He thinks he might move away. There are too many people concerned with the things he does and doesn't do. Too many people taking an interest when it's none of their business.

One day, he stops going to work entirely, stops trying to hold all the pieces together.

CHAPTER SEVEN

LEXI

Every inch of this town tells your story. From the playgrounds and schools to the street corners you hung out on with mates and the fields where you took your first sip of cider. It's a haven and a prison. It's full of ghosts; of joyful memories and heart-breaking ones; of hopes long extinguished. You've watched friends move away, for jobs and new beginnings; you've wished them well yet been envious. And you're still here. You chose to remain.

It could have been different. *Should* have been. The world is your oyster, they said—your parents—before they ruined everything.

That's not fair. You close your eyes briefly and ask for forgiveness.

Maybe you wouldn't have left, anyway. You love this place. You love the hills which make cycling and jogging an act of defiance, and the way Victorian terraces give way to the estates tacked on to the periphery, and the oldest houses—with thick stone walls and centuries-old ghosts—sit beside much newer builds.

You love the way the fields beyond town look deceptively close, and residential streets lead into thickets and one wrong turn finds you in a wooded valley and out into a creek.

Yet all of it is slowly disappearing. The mist has thickened to fog, obliterating the landscape. Upstream, the valley is no longer visible. The sprawling city suburbs across the river are gone.

Here, the sky remains cloudless and unblemished; the relentless sun is a warm sheet covering you as you doze on a stranger's lawn beneath a small apple tree, legs stretched out and crossed at the ankle. You've taken several smooth, palm-sized pebbles from the border without realizing. They're hot, burning into your skin. You put one on the grass and a second on top of it. It wobbles. You nudge it to keep it see-sawing—the movement, where there has been none for so long, is hypnotic. Another on top of that teeters, then settles. You scout around for more, becoming selective now, making sure the shape and size will complement the tower you've created.

This small task is satisfying. Nothing's dragging on your time. If you were at work, where you should be, phones would be ringing incessantly, paperwork would be dumped on your desk, and nothing would be good enough or fast enough for your line manager. You manage seven stones before the stack falls.

Yielding to the lethargy, your eyelids flutter to a close and your body is heavy. Your dreams are fragments, each scene a series of disparate images merging. The picture jerks like a silent movie from the 1900s. The faces are strangers.

Finn appears. Not quite him. A black-and-white staccato version. He's distant, staring at something you can't see, unaware of you.

"Finn!" You run forward to hug him, but there's something in the way he turns to look at you which makes you stop dead. Not even *at* you—*through* you, *past* you. As though you're in the way of the thing he actually wants to look at.

"You shouldn't be here." In one swift move, he grabs your T-shirt—it stretches and the fabric tears. Both of you are pulling and pushing at the same time. You try to coerce his fist open, but his grip is iron.

"You're hurting me. What are you doing? Let go of me."

Now you're in your own garden, and you've dragged Finn along too. Or vice versa. The stars twinkle, a veil of cloud drifts across a moon so bright it could be daytime. The black cat, the one from outside your house earlier, slinks through the undergrowth, its emerald eyes unblinking. It nuzzles your legs, but when you stoop to stroke it, it disappears, and you feel a wave of grief.

You rise into the air, floating above Finn and above the rooftops. Above people sleeping in their beds. Above a little girl watching you from her bedroom window. The sadness which enveloped you when you were on the ground falls away, the heaviness of it released, and you soar higher. You see the light of the sun and strive so hard to reach it.

Waking is disorientating. Briefly, you're relieved to be awake. And then you remember.

Thinking back over the dream, the details crumble until none of it is left.

"Oh, Finn ..."

With this imposed distance between you, your grievances seem petty and detached. His arms around you now would make everything better—his strong arms and muscular chest always do. Even the worst of arguments can be appeased when you take him by the hand and lead him upstairs.

How strange, the way life twists and turns. The moment before you met him, the second before he walked up to you in the pub that night, you were telling a friend you'd decided to quit your job and travel—your great big adventure before life bogged you down with babies and mortgages. All the grown-up stuff you wanted, but not yet. Tomorrow, you told your friend, you were booking the tickets.

You could barely keep still—bouncing on your toes as you reeled off all the countries you were hoping to visit. You'd been thumbing through travel magazines for months, the itinerary growing with each turn of the page. You were woozy with anticipation.

You were *so* close.

And then, there he was, in front of you.

"Hey, I'm Finn," he said, with the bravado of several pints coursing through him. "Can I buy you a drink?"

Gorgeous, sexy, heart-stopping. But you weren't looking to meet anyone, so you ignored the flush in your cheeks and flourished a hand towards the bar. "My friend's just getting me one, but thank you."

You turned away, but he remained beside you. You couldn't help taking a furtive peek, covering your face with your hand when he caught your eye.

He smiled victoriously. "The next one, then?"

In a split second, you'd considered the pros and cons. So many thoughts whizzing around, like a through-train on a deserted platform, leaving a vacuum in its wake. What harm could one drink do? Anyway, he'd be swept up by his mates and on to the next place before you'd even finished the drink you'd just started.

"Sure," you said.

Skip forward. You didn't travel. You talked about going together at some point, when you were certain where the relationship was heading. Finn surprised you with a few all-inclusive holidays to Mauritius and Barbados, as though that would be enough to soothe your appetite. He disliked leaving the hotel complex, with its staff ready to fulfil every whim and its sterile contrast to the enlivened landscape outside. You went on excursions, but never felt you saw the real country, and it rendered you dissatisfied. The urge to travel grew stronger, and Finn promised you would one day, but he got a promotion which meant more hours and more responsibility—he couldn't possibly leave until this big project was underway. And his father got ill, and his mum needed support.

You bought a house using the money set aside for traveling as the deposit.

"We'll top the account up quickly, but property's an investment—best to do it as soon as we can. I'll put this year's bonus straight into it. It'll be easier to save when we're not paying exorbitant rent."

No, instead you had exorbitant repair expenses, and replaced the double-glazing, and got a new car instead of a second-hand one.

You left *Wanderlust* and *Traveller* on the coffee table in the hope he'd be inspired. After a while, they grew a film of dust, and you threw them away with a tinge of regret. The man who swaggered up to you at the bar that night was exciting and spontaneous—how did he become so content in front of the TV with a takeaway?

More importantly, when did you allow him to drag you down with him?

Only last year you shook your head and said, "Sorry, I can't," when Mila suggested going to London to join the Extinction Rebellion demonstrations.

"Course you can, just tell him it's a girls' weekend."

"We don't lie to each other," you lied.

"Well, Cassie and I are going. You can still tag along, if you want to."

Jealousy stung you. Cassie was Mila's friend from the school run who Mila had started inviting to your girls' nights. She'd known her two years; you and Vanessa had barely known her six months. Yet, she was infiltrating the tight-knit friendship, organizing, taking over. A couple of times, you've suspected the three of them have met up without you.

They're probably doing so right now. Hardly noticing you've gone, in whatever alternate universe they are stranded in.

It's not them who are stranded, says a little voice you're trying to ignore.

The cat is suddenly brushing against your leg and for a moment you wonder if it's the cat whose voice you can hear. Anything's possible, right?

"You again? What's going on?" You reach for its collar, looking for a name, a contact number, a clue as to why it's following you around. It doesn't feel like a figment of your imagination, but at this moment—after all these hours and after no time at all—you're not entirely sure you can trust yourself.

Only a name is engraved.

You roll your eyes.

"Lucifer. Your name's Lucifer? I'd love to hear them calling you in the garden. I'm not calling you Lucifer. Luci, you're going to be Luci."

The cat winks and stretches out, moving his belly towards your hand for a tickle. You rest your head against the trunk of the apple tree and gaze along the road—the long, straight road, and the blanket of fog at the end of it.

CHAPTER EIGHT

FINN

Becoming a recluse is a strange thing. At some point, removing yourself from other people is the only way to survive. It may be a gradual process of societal withdrawal, over weeks or months until you lose track of the last time you went outside or heard someone else's voice. Or it could be a sudden trauma is the catalyst, a brick wall in the path which you're hurtling towards.

For Finn, it was a queue at the newsagent. They were talking about him when he walked in, their voices wafting along on the breeze. *Well, I heard she ...* with heads bowed together in their quest for gossip. They stopped abruptly when they saw him, the words stuck in their throats.

They were faces he recognized, but no one he knew. He walked up and down the shelves, gathering items, taking his time so he didn't have to encounter those prying eyes again too soon. When he joined the short queue, he stared straight ahead to deflect the whispers around him. A bristle of wariness lingered on the stale air.

A young girl of maybe four or five stood in front, turning to look at Finn with startled, unblinking eyes. He felt them boring into his soul. He tried to smile and make a silly face, the way Lexi would have, but he could tell the result was a distorted grimace.

Even as the kid's mother held her hand to pull her out of the path of other shoppers, she didn't stop gawking, oblivious to everything around her but Finn. The fear etched on her face grew deeper; Finn's skin crawled, turned inside out as though someone was scratching their nail down his spine.

The shop was airless—too far from either the coolness of the fridges or the freshness from the open door. The queue wasn't moving; sweat pooled along his hairline. He thought someone asked if he was okay, but he couldn't be sure. He wanted to leave, to drop his shopping and flee.

"Sophie."

The mother finally noticed what her daughter was doing, but the girl ignored all attempts to distract her. Finn turned his head, catching sight of himself in the CCTV feed above the counter, watching himself being watched.

"Sophie, come on." The mother moved to the front of the queue, paid for her items, and took the girl's arm. "I am so sorry," the mother said with embarrassment.

Finn nodded politely, looking at her properly for the first time—his next-door neighbor. Not the one who peeked from behind net curtains while her husband pottered in the garden, but the one prone to loitering at the end of her drive when anything juicy happened, such as when the police question residents about missing women. *This*, then, was the child who kicked balls against the fence with an annoying lack of rhythm, who cried at bedtime, who blew dandelion clocks onto his lawn.

It seemed she recognized him too, because she dragged her daughter away with additional urgency. "Sophie. Come on, *now.*"

The child broke her gaze and the two of them left. His hypnotism wore off as they walked down the road, and he could hear Sophie wailing, "But I wanted sweeties."

The assistant and other customers remained as detached as possible. Finn paid for his groceries, and the breeze when he reached it, was a relief.

He caught up with Sophie and her mother within a hundred paces—they were, after all, heading in the same direction, albeit at a much slower speed. He hung back to avoid further contact, but Sophie turned and continued to scrutinize him—pulled along by her mother while gazing behind.

Wherever he went after that day, people dodged him with increasing suspicion and wariness until it became easier to lock himself away.

***

Summer meanders into autumn. Finn contemplates the progression from his window, through the gaps in the curtains. Kids go back to school. Green trees turn brown; leaves litter his garden which is overgrown with weeds. The mornings are darker and dirtier; huge rainstorms move slowly from the west. Sunny mornings are tinged with a crisp bite. Finn spends far too many hours on his PlayStation. The vegetable seeds he planted rot without yielding anything edible.

One afternoon—Saturday, possibly—Vanessa bangs on the door. She crouches and peers through the letterbox while Finn sits on the stairs, half-way up, out of her line of vision. Her silhouette paces back and forth.

"I know you're there. Open the door, you coward."

He's holding one of Lexi's jumpers, salvaged from a rubbish bag all those months ago. He couldn't bear to part with everything, he realized.

"Where is she? Where's Lexi? It's been four months, and I haven't heard a thing from her." Her voice tails off, before: "Hiding won't do you any good, you know. You've got to come out eventually."

She beats her fist against the glass and Finn fears for its integrity, imagines it shattering and Vanessa falling through it with bloodied hands and a slash across her cheek. He'd have to sit her at the table and wash the debris from the wound. Each attack on the door is more aggressive than the last, echoing along the bare-walled hall, a crescendo of noise on the stagnant air.

"Oh, Finn," she sighs, her frenzy and anger finally abating. She rests her palms flat on the glass and presses her forehead between them. "I miss her so much. Where did she go?"

Finn hugs the jumper. It no longer has her fragrance—it's no more than a piece of tattered fabric now, stained with his tears. Crying is a new thing. He never thought himself capable.

"I just need to know."

"I'm sorry," Finn whispers.

***

The more he remains at home, the more the thought of leaving makes him sick. People study him, judge him, condemn him. He minimizes his time outside, but for some things it's unavoidable. Huddled in his jacket, with a scarf wrapped around his face, he walks with his head down to repel attention. His once substantial demeanor—an unstoppable flanker on the rugby pitch—reduced to an outline.

"It's all in your head, mate," Dean says. "No one's watching you. No one cares."

They talk on the phone now; Finn hasn't been to the pub in weeks. Dean's come over a couple of times, but Finn was on edge for the whole of it.

"Did you go to the doctor?" Dean asks. Another day, another conversation. Wheedling out information Finn is reluctant to give.

"Anxiety. A bit of depression. She gave me tablets."

"And you're taking them?"

Finn's attention is caught by two birds flitting around the garden, pecking for worms, fighting over the juiciest.

"Mate, you can't bury your head. If you've been given pills, take them."

"I guess."

"I've got to go. Nat's waiting for me."

"Next week? You'll phone next week?"

Dean sighs on the end of the line. "Yeah. Take care, mate."

Kids walk along the road dressed as witches and superheroes. He turns off his light in case a stray one finds their way to his door trick-or-treating. Fireworks whizz through the air. Christmas lights appear on the front of houses and trees are decorated in the windows. Finn is gradually absorbed into the walls.

His boss rings at the beginning of each month. Not Rachel—that would be easy—no, the big boss who rarely deals with the staff. It used to be HR who called, but The Boss has taken over. "You need another sick note, or we'll have to work towards a phased return. We can't afford to keep the job open much longer.

Finn sneers. They can, they just don't *want* to.

The police phone intermittently, keeping him updated on their progress, of which there's none. With no discernible lead, there's little they can do. Lexi's photo is still circulated. She hasn't been forgotten, they assure him.

Finn knows she hasn't because she's everywhere he turns. Every time he wakes, and she isn't beside him; every time he walks down the stairs and into another empty room. She's the movement in the corner of his eye, the monster in his wardrobe or under the bed.

"The thing is, Mr. Carmichael, she could be anywhere. Some people don't always want to be found. If she was of sound mind—"

"She was."

"—the obvious assumption is she chose to leave."

In the kitchen, he opens the fridge and scans the scant shelves. It's lunchtime but he's not hungry. "I'm sorry for wasting your time. Phoebe ..." He takes a bottle of lager and stares at it. "She meant well, I guess. I don't know what she expected. We should never have got you involved."

"You did the right thing, sir. Should any further information come to light, please don't hesitate to contact us."

"Thank you."

Mostly, it's Phoebe herself who calls, although less frequently and more randomly than before. He sighs heavily when her name flashes up on the screen, leaving it longer and longer each time before answering. It's the same question again and again.

"Anything?"

"I'm sorry, Phoebe—you know I'd call if there was news."

She huffs. "I still can't accept it. She's strong. She's not the type to run away."

Can it be classed as running away when you're thirty? "Perhaps it's time we let go."

"How can I, Finn? She's all I've got."

"I'm sorry." He's drained. He has nothing left to offer her. When he hangs up, he vows it'll be the last time he speaks to her.

***

People scuttle along in brightly colored bobble hats and gloves. It snows. It rains. On some days, the sky's clear and the sun shines brightly on the frost. The roofs of cars glisten with intricate patterns.

Finn's boss phones, and Finn finally agrees to resign—an easy acquiescence, as it turns out. He's surprised to discover he's more relaxed without the worry of his job hanging over him than he has been for a long time. The proverbial weight on your shoulders is perhaps real, after all. Instead of waking with niggling trepidation that he ought to be at work, he rolls over and goes back to sleep.

He sells his car to pay the bills, however—the last thing of value he owns. Once his pride and joy, now only an unused ornament on his drive. The local garage facilitates the transaction and deposits the money into his account. Finn can't watch as the mechanic drives it away. He listens to the purr of the engine as it peters out into the distance.

It snows again, then rains. A huge storm and gale-force winds break branches from the trees at the back of the house and block the narrow alley. Tiles slide from roofs, but not his. Sophie's dad from next door jumps over the wall into Finn's garden to retrieve a trampoline.

Days get longer. The clocks change.

Finn stands in the middle of the room and the world spins beneath him. He pictures the planet hurtling through space; he feels the momentum holding him in place.

It rains less. It's sunny more often. He wears T-shirts instead of jumpers.

The house slowly clears itself. As items break or become superfluous, they're discarded and not replaced. He only needs one mug, after all. One plate, one set of cutlery. The rest of Lexi's things are boxed up and stored in the attic—her photos and paintings bought from market stalls and little ornaments of sheep, fluffy throws and cushions, books. The house resonates in a vaguely metallic way.

Sometimes he finds something new—a scarf tucked among his jeans, a lipstick wedged between the sofa cushions. Things which seem to appear rather than having been overlooked. He shivers when he touches them, these persistent pieces of her.

CHAPTER NINE

LEXI

You're dead. Of course you are. Not sitting on a cloud gazing down at humanity dead. Not comfortably lying six feet beneath the ground in a silk-lined coffin dead. You're drifting in this limbo state, unable to escape, unsure what to do next. Perhaps you should be repenting, acknowledging your sins. What sins? The argument you had with Finn last night—does that count? It was nothing, surely—nothing worse than anything which has gone before.

The sin of selfishness or laziness, of greed. Of taking sickies that even Finn doesn't know about and traveling to Exeter for the day. Of harboring thoughts that Finn isn't the man you want to spend the rest of your life with.

Or possibly not dead, but in a coma. Tied to wires in a hospital bed, with nurses checking your vital signs periodically and giving comfort to Finn who's holding vigil beside you. His face pallid and drawn through worry and lack of sleep, allowing only a bleak smile when someone enters the room and suggests he goes down to the café for a sandwich. *You need to stay strong for Lexi.*

Coma indicates calamity, but you don't remember. You have a vague grasp of falling, of weightlessness. But without context, the image is nothing.

If not a coma, then you're simply sleeping. All of this is a single, fractious dream. And when you wake to the buzz of your alarm clock on Midsummer's Day, this will be a fleeting aside. You'll tell Finn you had the strangest dream, but when you search for the details, they'll falter and evaporate.

Once more, you're adrift. Once more, or simply *still?* Your watches remain at 6:05, and the sun hugs the rooftops. It should be climbing high overhead by now—lunchtime, or just past it, perhaps. You're not hungry, so maybe it's not as late as you think. On a normal day, with time nudging you into fixed, structured segments, you'd have made coffee to drink at your desk and opened a new packet of chocolate digestives. The thought of food is making you nauseous.

It's all a bit boring really. Perhaps you should go to the pub. You could get drunk, pass out, wake up in your own bed, or someone else's. Or run naked down Fore Street. Or write swear words on the whiteboards at the primary school. Or ...

You could smash the windows, *all of them*; raid the supermarket freezers for their Rocky Road; steal a boat from the jetty and sail away.

But you don't do any of that—would it make any difference if you did? Are they real ice-creams and windows? Would there be consequences? You remain where you are, staring up a road where you literally just stopped walking at some point. You're slipping into yourself. Heavy air presses down on you. Your mind empties.

When you were little, your mum always told you not to move from where you were if you lost sight of her. "Stay put," she'd say, "and I'll come back and find you."

If you move, was her inference, you'd be gone forever.

Oh Mum ...

A tear slides down your cheek.

You keep her submerged, usually, in the deep recesses of your memory—her and your father alike. They were stolen from you, far too early. You were eighteen when a drunk driver ploughed into them on New Year's Eve. They went out and never came back. You returned from the pub to find the police waiting for you, and you had to comprehend the tragedy and seriousness after too many vodka and cokes.

A lot of people don't know that. Acquaintances, work colleagues—they all share so much of themselves, and yet you hold back. It's not important, you'd say; it doesn't define you. But that misses the point. Vanessa and ... the woman with the kids ... Mila!—they both know, of course. Friends who spent half their primary school years sleeping on your bedroom floor or bundling into the back of your dad's car to go to the trampoline club. They sat in church for the funeral, just as awkward and incongruous as you felt.

Finn had no idea you were an orphan until your first Christmas together when he queried why there weren't decorations in the house and asked if you wanted to invite your parents. There'd been no reason to mention it before, it was never relevant. He was dismayed when you explained, hurt you'd hidden it from him.

"No, not hidden," you said. Not *hidden* at all. Managing the pain, perhaps; attempting a semblance of normality. Endeavoring to prevent yourself from being engulfed and overwhelmed by a distress you couldn't control.

"I'm sorry," you said, managing his resentment. It's not the way around it ought to have been.

A stone gets caught under your foot and bounces in front of you. When you reach it, you kick it again, keeping it slightly in front of you as you scuff and shuffle along, until you get bored. You pick it up and squeeze until it digs into your palm and leaves little jagged imprints.

You haven't been to their grave in months, maybe longer. There's no excuse except life moves on. Eleven years—is that too soon to forget?

They left you. And you hated them. Young and bitter and irrational. Unable to deal with the residual emotions. Why them and not ... Vanessa's parents who were on the verge of divorce and spent half the time ignoring her? Why not the couple in their seventies who wore matching hats and coats, and held hands as they walked down the road? Why not someone, anyone else?

You place the stone on the low wall outside the police station. This is your mother. You hunt the grass verge for others, digging into the dust-dry earth to free them. A solid compact one for your father. The third, placed on top, is your fury and frustration. You keep hold of your angular grief.

The cemetery is overgrown and as parched as the rest of town. Long grasses curl around the gravestones and monuments; weeds creep across the paths. You hadn't meant to come, but perhaps this is the only place to be.

As you shuffle along, you note headstones for babies and for octogenarians; some where the lettering has faded to almost nothing at all, and graves so new they're still marked with small wooden crosses, and the flowers are funeral fresh.

And here they are, to the right and two plots over. Your steps are tentative, as if sneaking home long after curfew.

Each time you visit, you half-expect their grave not to be here, still wishing it's a vivid nightmare which has seeped into the daytime. Hoping they're waiting for you in the stunning river-view flat they moved into after selling the family home. Berating you for being later than you said you'd be, and you having to explain you went to the cemetery by mistake. And you'd laugh because you miss the sound of their laughter.

"Hello, Mum. Hello, Daddy."

Your voice is tight and hollow. You purse your lips to prevent the pain trickling out. You sit cross-legged on the edge of the plot and rest your palm on the grass, picturing their coffins being lowered into the ground and the mourners gathered around you in a tight knot. You're standing at the open grave, soil in hand but unable to throw it in. Phoebe takes your hand and guides you.

At the base of the stone, decorative pebbles hide the plastic plant pots dug into the soil; the plot itself is devoid of the weeds and scruffiness of its neighbors. Phoebe must come and tend to it, but she's never said. She's never knocked on your door and invited you to join her. Your mother was her younger sister, someone she spent years protecting and looking out for. But when it mattered most, there was nothing she could do.

Phoebe selected the black granite headstone, taking time to consider the gold versus silver lettering. She took you with her, but the number of options was overwhelming, and you found yourself staring at a broken, half-engraved stone abandoned against the side of the workshop. The wording, too, was her choice: *Roger Peters and his wife Bryony Peters. Together always.*

73

You take one of the pebbles in your hand, smooth and pure white—the kind you buy in a shop rather than dig up from the beach. You fidget with it, twisting and turning between your fingers.

"I'm sorry I haven't come to see you recently. I ..." You stop, wondering what adolescent excuse will pour from your mouth. Words disintegrate.

The lettering on the headstone catches the sunlight and dances. *Roger* catches your eye and blinds you for a moment. When you close your eyes, you see his name flashing in front of you.

Death scares you. More specifically, your power over it. You'd been arguing with your mum—something futile and Christmas-magnified, though you don't fully recall. But you were eighteen and impetuous, so it was obviously important because everything was.

"Why can't you just leave me alone? This is *my* life!"

Days later, they did.

All these graves, all these people. Were they wished away too?

You move to get comfortable and settle against the headstone, legs stretched out, and imagine the hot granite is your dad's arms around you, the way you'd curl up on the sofa to watch *Toy Story* together when you were six.

"I wish you could have met Finn—you'd have loved him, Dad. He could have taken you to the rugby, and you'd have had someone to talk about carburetors with." A smile is fleeting on your lips.

"And I wish you could see the person I grew into, the woman you made me. People aren't whole when they're eighteen, are they? They think they are, but there's so much left to do. I wish

I'd gone to the party with you instead of out with my friends. That was the plan, wasn't it, to meet up with the family? But I thought it would be boring. If I'd been there, we'd have left later and someone else ..."

Someone else may have died. You'd have driven past the crumpled car on the way home or been diverted by POLICE INCIDENT signs.

You rest your head back and sigh, unsure what else there is to say. The tops of the trees strike out into the blue sky; the sun catches on the leaves making them sharply luminous. And yet, across the valley, at the apex of the opposite hill, with its pastel-painted houses heaped on top of each other, the fog is descending; the streets are filled as if it were a river gushing out to sea.

"Everything was okay yesterday. I ..." Memories fail; you admit defeat. Yesterday is so long ago. "We're having a brutal heatwave. Do you remember the one when I was little? The reservoir dried up and we walked around the edge inside it, didn't we?"

As with today, the heat back then was relentless. The collective enthusiasm for the initial good spell slowly dripped away like sweat on the nape of your neck. Impossible to sleep at night, to concentrate at school, to do anything other than lie down with the curtains shut and the windows open so the fabric got sucked outside. Someone on TV claimed you could fry an egg on the pavement, so you tried it. It didn't work. Your dad found you washing gloopy yolk from the patio.

"This is hotter."

You stare at the fog even though you don't want to, even though you want to pretend it's not there. Despite the heat, you're chilled when you look at it.

"They're all gone. Everyone. I've been looking for them. I've tried my best."

The fog is moving towards you. Still far off, still with hundreds of houses and many roads and lanes between you. But coming.

"Mummy. Wouldn't I know if I was dead?"

It's such an absolute word. Whatever *this* is, it doesn't feel absolute. It feels *next*. Like a journey, slowly heading onwards. How can something so slow and languorous be the end? At your age, death would be nothing other than horrific. Surely, you'd remember such a thing.

You never had time to cultivate beliefs about death—you're not religious, so the idea of heaven and hell are just stories. Your parents were there, then they weren't. You didn't have time to consider the theological implications—you were focused on the confusion and loneliness, the gaping hole ripped into you. You avoided discussions about reincarnation or ghosts or how any of this fits together, and in those drunken, late-night musings, you'd be the one to say, "When you're dead, you're dead," and the conversation would lapse.

Finn's a good man. He won't let you die. He'll keep searching until he finds you and brings you home.

CHAPTER TEN

FINN

It's the longest day of the year again. The longest day of the longest year.

People are converging on Stonehenge to celebrate the summer solstice. In Austria, they'll be lighting bonfires on mountaintops to ward off bad spirits, and dancing around maypoles in Sweden. In the Arctic Circle, the sun won't set at all today.

And here's Finn. In the calm chill of the pre-dawn hours, wide-eyed and reflective.

Because it's the longest day again. A whole year since Lexi—

He stops himself, catches her name as though it's a leaf on the breeze and scrunches it in his fist.

How has it been a year? It feels, equally, much shorter and much longer, as if he's just sat down, as if he's been frozen in place for centuries, enduring the torture and desolation. He's devoid of all thought, yet bombarded by a thousand images. Her perfume fills the room; her breath catches on his neck; her body presses into the curve of his back. For a second, it seems the last twelve months have been a single, elongated nightmare.

There's a tightness when he thinks of her. In his chest, in his stomach. His antidepressants have kept her memory at bay over the past few months, but the doctor is lowering the dose, easing him off them and her face is returning. What he'd give for one more kiss, one more conversation. It would become a fight, it always did. He'd blame her for whatever *this* is that he's turned into, this shell; and she'd laugh. She'd always laugh.

In the bathroom, he splashes cold water on his face. He's going grey. Not just his hair, but his skin and eyes too. Color leeching away from him.

The phone rings and he winces. The landline. Phoebe. The only person who uses that number barring cold callers selling insulation and solar panels.

"Hello."

"Have you heard anything?"

"No."

There's a protracted sigh. "I was so sure. I thought, today of all days ..." Phoebe exhales shakily. "It's harder to keep hoping, isn't it?"

Finn nods but can't find words of comfort. He's said it all before; it's unfeasible to retain the same level of sincerity.

"How are you doing?" she asks as his silence expands.

"Okay."

"Have you found a new job?"

"No."

"Don't you think it's time?" Pause. "Sorry. Not my place."

"It's been so long, I'm not sure I can." He peers through the curtains, drawing the edge back with one finger and blinking at the sunlight. The room remains dark, comforting.

"What would Lexi say, if she came home and saw you like this? You can't put your life on hold forever."

Does a year mean he should be over it? How long is too long to mourn someone who went away? "You can talk!"

"I'm an old woman—it's my prerogative. You're not even forty yet—you're in the prime of your life, so they say. Are you going to sit alone and wait to die? It's not what Lexi would want for you."

***

It's not even midday when Finn opens a bottle of lager and tries to stop Lexi infiltrating his head. Lager, cider, coffee vodka liqueur. The dregs of red wine in the back of the cupboard. The dusty bottle of Jack Daniel's. They're all in his sights.

He drinks to forget Phoebe's disapproving tone, and Dean's exasperation and abruptness when he phones these days.

The air is languid, the heat rises. Another sizzling summer. *Climate change*, he thinks, glumly. Anomalous heatwaves are a thing of the past—searing summers are expected now. At some point, it'll all be far too hot.

He sits on the back doorstep, making the most of the cooling gusts of wind. From several gardens over, the noise of a barbeque floats across—bubbling conversations with sporadic laughter and the piercing tones of kids running and shrieking. It's too much—too loud, too boisterous and unpredictable. Not safe. Nothing's safe.

On this step, he's cocooned within the walls of the house, protected from the gossip and accusations which Dean says don't exist. A couple of strides further out and anyone glancing from their back bedroom window would spot him, these hateful people who surround him.

"You're being paranoid, mate." Dean says over and over. Or did, until the last few times Finn's called, when he's made some lame excuse not to talk, or not picked up and forced Finn to leave a voicemail.

It's the word the doctor used when she hesitated over the next prescription and decided to halve the dosage.

The afternoon mutates into the evening. Empty bottles appear on the dining table. The sun sets in a pinkish-purple glow—a vibrant twilight which will extend all the way to dawn, skipping the darkest part of the night altogether. The light from the kitchen creates a long shadow of Finn's body. When he stands, it stretches half-way down the garden, his distorted head reaching Lexi's vegetable patch.

He steps forward, far enough from the house he can't touch the wall for reassurance. In a half-thought, he wonders if it will disappear completely if he wanders too far and won't be able to find his way back. Things go missing in this house—important letters, his favorite T-shirt, people. Why not the house itself?

Someone from the barbeque starts to strum a slow version of 'Living on a Prayer'. Shit. He'd forgotten he wasn't alone. The guests lapse into silence. The only sound is the guitar.

Another step.

Finn's hand begins to tremble, shaking up the contents of his glass, but he forces himself to stay, there in his garden on this pleasant summer evening. Just a minute longer, maybe two.

The man he was when he met Lexi six years ago—hell, the man she left behind last year—wouldn't have given up. Wouldn't have deferred to these ridiculous fears. He'd have faced them, punched them into a wall.

"This is what you did," he mutters. "This is what happened when you went."

With another sip of Jack, ice clinking against the side of the glass, his vision blurs. Always one sip too far. He stares into the golden whiskey and sees her face. He looks at the shadows of the leylandii and sees her there too.

"I lost my job," he tells Lexi. "You always hated me working so much, never cared about the money. Well, guess what? I don't have any anymore. I stay at home and think about you."

The party's breaking up with loud farewells. A flurry of activity, then the lights are off and there's silence.

"I don't know what to do next. I don't know where to start." He looks down at his feet on the grass. *This* is where it starts. He turns on the spot and looks up at the trees bordering the alley at the bottom of the garden, then at the house—tired and unkempt, a sheen of green algae on the white walls, windows in need of cleaning.

Sophie—the little girl next door—watches warily from her bedroom window, as unsettling as that day in the shop. They lock eyes. She gasps and retreats into her room; a chill runs down his spine. Her shadow dances on the curtains for a moment, taunting him, reminding him she's there and she's still watching.

"This has got to stop." He downs his drink and smashes the glass against the house. The residue dribbles down the wall.

***

Through the agony of a throbbing head and gritty mouth, Finn tries to make sense of the day before. He leans over the sink and tries to swallow paracetamol. He fumbles for his phone and calls Dean.

Unusually, Dean answers within three rings.

"Hey."

"Mate, you sound awful. What's up?"

"Hangover."

"Not good to drink alone."

"It's been a year."

"Ah."

Surely he knows that. Surely the date is seared into everyone's heads.

"So, you thought you'd get bladdered?"

"Didn't have anything else to do. I tried to call—thought you could come over."

"Yeah, sorry. Nat broke her arm—I've been cooking and dealing with the kids, as well as trying to get to work on time."

"Right."

"Look, it's not the best time—"

"I was wondering—"

Dean inhales. "The thing is." Exhales. "I know you've been through a lot, with Lexi and all, but hiding away ain't helping. People break up all the time—they don't … Nat thinks I'm enabling you—her word, not mine. She thinks you've got to help yourself now, that I can't do it for you." He clears his throat. "You understand, right? That I can't always be there? I've got to go, so I'll see you round, yeah."

Finn listens to the silence Dean leaves behind. He slams the phone onto the table. "That's *why* I was fucking *calling!*"

What the hell does Dean's wife know about it anyway? Lexi never liked her—tolerated her, made polite conversation when she had no choice, but avoided her if she could. She jumped over a table to get away, once! And here she is, Nat, claiming to be some bloody expert and discern what's best for him!

Enabling. Finn can hear the scorn when she says it, can hear the venom. Fine. You know what? He doesn't need Dean. He doesn't need anyone.

He's at his study door before he knows it. He hasn't been in here for months. It smells musty, so he opens the window. The letters and bills and other detritus on the desk tell the story of a completely different man. He crosses his fingers his laptop will switch on after so long.

He stares at the screen, hovering the cursor over the email icon, deciding against opening it and considering deleting it and creating a new account entirely. Apps and files pinned to the desktop are alien. His fingers on the keyboard are stale and clumsy. He searches for a job site and stares at the list of options.

It was short-sighted to think he could carry on this way. Phoebe was right—he can't spend the next forty years tucked away, scrimping for money. There are pennies left in his savings, a couple of months' worth at best. It used to be all about the money when he was younger—seeing the balance dripping away would have devastated him. Now, he couldn't care less.

Another thing Lexi had a hand in, presumably. She wasn't swayed by his job title or his money. She loved him. Until she didn't anymore.

"Enough," he whispers.

He scrolls through shelf-stacking and warehouse jobs, cleaning and delivery driving jobs. Jobs where he can put his head down and get on with it, turn up and go home at the end of the day. He baulks at putting on a shirt and tie again—his suits hang in the wardrobe, ghosts of his previous life—yet, a week later, he's dressed up for an interview for a part-time job in a solicitor's office.

"To be honest, Mr. Carmichael, you've got all the prerequisites for the job, but I'm a little surprised you're not seeking a more prominent position, given your experience and previous employment." She leans back in her chair and smiles. "We're looking for someone who will commit to the company in the long-term."

Finn focuses on his hands resting in his lap, trying to prevent himself fidgeting. "As you can see from my CV, Miss Anderson, I've had some time out, for personal reasons. I'm no longer looking for the type of work I did previously."

Miss Anderson glances back to his application. "Oh, yes, I see that now. Oh, you're ..." She blushes distinctly and stares at the paper in front of her. "Of course, I'm aware of the circum-stances ... I—I'm sorry for your ..." She takes a breath and moves quickly in another direction. "Um, so, the job will involve some book-keeping as well as general admin work. We're looking for someone for three days a week, in the first instance, but hours may increase down the line."

Finn nods, and after a couple more questions, she wraps up the interview. They stand to shake hands. He receives a call offering him the job before he's even made his way home.

CHAPTER ELEVEN

LEXI

You run through the names of your friends. They're starting to lose cohesion.

Mila, who lives close and has kids and a flighty ex-husband, who wants to save the planet and reprimands you—gently—when you buy something ensnared in plastic. Vanessa, who delves into the bottom of a tin to eat the chocolates everyone else avoids, who gives the best advice and makes the most amazing carrot cake, and who won't let you wallow in self-pity, no matter what the reason.

There's someone missing. You've forgotten someone.

You close your eyes and picture yourself at a table in a pub. It was your birthday and all four of you were having dinner— Mila, Vanessa, you, and …

A balloon with *30* emblazoned upon it is tied to your chair. *She* brought it, the one whose name is on the tip of your tongue. Her bag's slung across the back of her chair, her glass half-full. Her red lipstick has left tiny traces on the rim.

She exists. But she's not in your head. You want to grab hold of her hand and prevent her from disappearing. But you don't know her anymore. The fog has caught up with her, and she's gone.

Is that what it's doing? Devouring everything you know piece by piece?

Finn remains—although he's beginning to feel like a distant memory, someone from long ago. When you close your eyes, his features are shadowy, as though you're peering at him in a darkened room. He's beside you and yet so far away.

You think about the silly notes he leaves you, and the caramel color of his eyes, and the day you met. You recall his hesitation when you closed in for your first kiss, despite his swagger in approaching you. He was gentle, almost shy.

The first kiss. The taste of lager on his lips, the static shock of his hand on your spine. His firm yet tender touch. His intense gaze as you stumbled apart. You tremble, as you did then, catching your breath. You conjure his woody, spicy aftershave, because you don't want Finn to be engulfed and forgotten.

Finn would hate this idling around, you know that much. He'd hate the lethargy and the heat. He'd be on his feet, dragging you this way or that, looking for the way out, the answer.

But you've already found the answer. Now, idling around seems to be all there is left.

***

It's 6:05 when you make the decision to walk across the bridge. When you decide to face the fog head-on and stride through it to the other side. When you realize you have no choice. You have to know what's there; you can't keep imagining or hoping.

You could still be wrong—the whole town could still be crouched behind hedges and cars, wedged into all the tiny spaces with their fingers on their lips to stifle giggles, waiting for you to find them. It's 6:05. They've only been hiding for a moment.

There are little piles of stones along your route that you have no recollection of creating. They sit atop postboxes and bins, and on benches and walls. With no one to disturb them, they remain perfectly balanced. A small nudge or gust of wind would have them tumbling into a heap.

The fog obliterates whole roads, concealing the hills and the schools and the houses and everything inside them. But you look ahead and pay no heed because you're going to be free of it soon. There's a slight skip in your step, a lightness you haven't felt for a long time. Your exuberance bubbles just below the surface.

At the top of Fore Street, you waver. The framework of the two bridges looms into view. The towers and suspension cables of the road bridge, and the wrought iron arcs of the rail bridge, are ethereal through the fog, reminiscent of the pencil sketches sold in several of the gift shops. These bridges have a long relationship with river fog.

"Not this fog though. This one's brand new."

Goosebumps bristle along your arm; your fists clench instinctively as you steel yourself.

"I can do this." Your voice is tiny compared to the bellows that emanated when you were going from house to house, knocking on your neighbors' doors, convinced someone would answer.

You walk guardedly past dark and abandoned shops, past the trees and traffic lights, past the pub, and the other pub. You don't run or skip or stride now. Each step is measured, controlled. And here you are, standing at the end of the bridge, peering into the abyss. About a third of the way along, it disappears.

On a normal day, the bridge vibrates with lorries speeding across. It shakes and hums, the metal girders underneath creak and strain. If you look down on a normal day, the river is thick with silt. Today, the water is serene and colorless. That's not right. You see all the way to rainbow-colored pebbles on the riverbed, boats on the surface seem to be floating in mid-air. That's not right either.

A third of the way across, the river too is swallowed.

Faltering steps propel you forward. You cling to the railing to prevent yourself bottling out. Why so scared? This is your decision. You *need* to do this, but at the same time there's nothing you want to do less. The idea of this peaceful existence being ruined is perturbing; the possibility of crowds and their mayhem tumbling back into this dormant world unnerves you. It's been too long without them. How long? How does time pass when it's evidently not passing? From this spot on the bridge, the sun is hidden by the fog, and for the first time today you feel cooler, almost cold.

You've moved closer. Or the fog has advanced towards you. Water vapor transforms into droplets which trickle down your arm and cling to the tips of your fingers. Deep within, the fog crackles with lightning and grumbles like the voices of a million people. You press your palm against it—dense and viscous, as though it could support your weight if you leant against it. Fine tentacles coil around your fingers.

It grips you gently, like a mother encouraging a child away. It lures you with compassion. The tarmac is gone from under you, your feet are inches from the surface. Held close by these invisible arms, you're enveloped by the ice-solid air.

And you realize, there's no *other side*. Just a bottomless chasm. There's no one waiting to come pouring back, no one expecting you. You're still alone.

You're tired. Eyes fluttering, limbs loose and malleable. Allowing the fog to overcome you. Giving up, because there's no one to fight for, and you no longer have the desire. How easy to simply slip away.

And in this swirling white fog, you imagine Finn. Softly smiling, the way he always does when he looks at you, his eyes full of love and longing.

"I'm not ready," you whisper.

Slowly, the hands loosen. The fog withdraws to a near distance, leaving you depleted and exposed on the bridge.

Once more, the tarmac burns into you, the ferocity returns. The thunderous noises from the fog have abated; all sound is lost again. The sky is deep and infinite, without a blemish or wrinkle. You don't move. You have all the time you could ever need.

You miss the darkness and the shape of the stars and the relief of the sun setting and the streaks of purple and orange that ebb away.

When you were little, your dad would take you to the field beside the secondary school on the hill. You lived on the other side of town, then, so he'd bundle you into the car in a fluffy blanket and take you on an adventure. You were above the orange glow of streetlights and when you looked up, you felt closer to the sky than the ground beneath you.

You'd curl into him, staring at the pinpricks of light which, he explained, were millions of miles away, and the shapes they made were called the Hunter and the Little Bear even though they looked nothing like those things.

You often fell asleep on that patch of grass, cuddled into Daddy to keep warm, and he'd carry you to the car and then to bed. In the morning, you were never completely certain if it had been real or not.

***

You miss the darkness.

You miss people banging into you because they're staring at their phones.

You miss waiting to cross a road streaming with traffic, and politely saying hello to the people you walk past.

You miss the shiver when you turn a corner into the wind. You miss the wind—the way a waft tussles your hair because it's too fine to hold in place, or a gust snags the cherry blossom and sets pink petals free like confetti, or a gale pounds into you and knocks you off your feet.

You miss the vapor trails of long-haul flights. And birdsong filling the air with melody. So, you sing to fill the disconcerting vacuum. A whisper to begin with, the lyrics barely brushing your lips. Nonsense rhymes about being alone or about the grass being yellow, not green, because all the songs you used to know are draining from your memory.

You miss Finn. You miss the hope you had everything would be normal again.

CHAPTER TWELVE

FINN

Finn's new job suits him. He arrives an hour after everyone else and leaves two hours earlier. At lunchtime, a snatched fifteen-minute break—which hardly matters during such a short day—he gazes down on Fore Street from his first-floor window. Pockets of people swarm from their buildings, their offices or shops, to buy lunch or take a breather in the sunshine. They chat with friends or sit briefly on the bench opposite Finn's window before slinking back through the doors which leads to other businesses above the shops. Choreographed lives, moving in sync. Finn has been outside of these established routines for so long, it all seems so regimented and humdrum.

He starts to recognize people who walk past regularly, giving them puerile nicknames: Bungle, Jogging Man, Giant Hat Lady.

Sometimes he sees Lexi, except he doesn't, of course. He leans forward, following her progress down the street, until his forehead presses against the glass, and she disappears.

"Are you all right there?" asks his colleague, a lady in her late fifties with dyed auburn hair and glasses on a chain around her neck.

"Yes." He straightens up and turns back to his desk. She wants an explanation, gossip to pass on later, so he doesn't give her one.

Beneath his keyboard is a piece of paper with two names scribbled on it, *Bea* and *Ingrid;* jotted down on his first day because he knew he'd forget. This is Ingrid. He crosses paths with Bea rarely because they work on different days. The three of them form the admin team. It's a small office, six of them since Finn and a new solicitor joined.

"Coffee? I'm putting the kettle on."

"No, thank you."

"How are you getting on with everything? Are you settling in okay?"

"Fine." Pause, awkward and looming. "Thank you."

He's forgotten how to converse with people, how to make polite small talk to fill the day and the silences. He's suspicious of Ingrid's casual chatter while she peers over the top of her computer monitor. He's sure she remembers the headlines. The smaller he makes himself, the easier it'll be for her to overlook him.

It's a twenty-minute stroll to work; slightly longer on the way home with the weight of the day clinging to him. Sometimes the sky is so big he needs to hold on to something to prevent being sucked up and away. He catches his reflection in the windows of houses as he passes, a scared old man muttering to himself. Not old. He turned thirty-nine when he wasn't paying attention. This isn't how he imagined his life would turn out.

He's sure people are still talking about him, but when he glances at them—when passing them in the street or sitting opposite them at the doctor's surgery—they stare resolutely ahead and pretend not to notice him. He imagines their discussions later: *Guess who I saw today? That weird guy whose girlfriend vanished! Something dodgy there, if you ask me.* He digs his hands into his pockets and squeezes his keys so hard they pierce the skin.

Maybe he should have moved after all, started afresh. But how would Lexi know where to come back to?

***

To avoid seeing the same people day after day, each following their own strict schedules and timings, Finn takes detours. He goes via the park, or out to the crossroads and back up past the fire station. He walks through the woods in the deep valley between one housing estate and another—an area he thought was a secret until he noticed the benches and freshly painted fairy houses for kids.

Today he finds himself outside the glass-fronted library. It's not the first time he's come this way, but the first he's paused to watch people browsing the shelves or sitting at tables with newspapers. He's fascinated by the level of deliberation in choosing a book—the way they tilt their head to read the spine, the gentle way they ease the book from its tightly-packed neighbors. Each seems content in their own company.

He goes in. He hadn't meant to. He hasn't read a book in years; he's not even sure he's a member. No one looks up to stare, the way they do in pubs. The atmosphere is welcoming but unobtrusive.

The high ceiling causes an echo when someone clears their throat, or a stack of books is placed on the trolley. On the mezzanine floating above his head, there's an art exhibition and someone giving a talk to seven or eight people, tightly gathered so the speaker doesn't have to project her voice too far.

Despite the signage declaring FICTION and LOCAL HISTORY and COOKERY, Finn is uncertain where he wants to be. He shuffles across the room and scans a noticeboard full of details of clubs and activities. No, too many people to consider something like that. He picks up a newspaper instead and sits at the table nearest the exit. He doesn't read; he merely flips the pages and pretends. He regrets coming in. After a few minutes, he leaves.

The silence and cool cordiality, however, were comforting, and the following Tuesday he's there again, not socializing, but close enough. He finds himself returning the subsequent Tuesdays, simply by not making the decision to walk a different route. Baby steps back to normality.

He snorts a little at *normality*—at no point in his life has he considered regular attendance in a library *normal*.

The same faces are there each time, all in their favorite spots, which makes his visits more relaxed. It means there are no surprises. The Knit and Natter group chat merrily and share homemade cakes. A guy with a lever-arch folder teeming with loose pages sits at one of the computers banked against the far wall. A woman with a shopping trolley unloads her maximum allowance and resolutely heads to find more—working her way, Finn comes to notice, through the shelves in alphabetical order.

The staff begin to make conversation. They walk past his table and make remarks about the weather or the headline he's reading. He knows their names because of the badges pinned to their shirts: Jon and Amber and Deborah.

Today, Amber says, "Someone's run off with the Guardian, I'm afraid, if you're looking for it. You'll have to make do with something else."

"Ah well, it's all the same rubbish anyway, isn't it?"

"Maybe you should try a book?"

"I'm not much of a reader."

She's standing beside the NEW ARRIVALS display. She trails a finger along the covers, either not hearing him or ignoring him. She pulls two hardbacks from their stands, proffering them to Finn. "What about a thriller?"

Both covers have women staring at him with steely vacant expressions, albeit appearing delicate and fragile at the same time. One has a shoulder-length bob with a fringe falling into her eyes; the other, a ruby-red lipstick smirk.

Both remind him of Lexi.

He recoils. "Ah. No."

His voice is louder and more abrupt than he expected. Amber snatches the books back, blushing with confusion.

"I'm sorry," he says weakly. "But, um, thank you."

She smiles tightly, returns the books to the shelf, and disappears through the door marked STAFF ONLY.

Finn kicks the table leg in annoyance. Lexi again! Lurking in his head, refusing to relinquish her grasp on him. How much longer will he have to suffer? How many more days and nights will she fill his thoughts?

On Friday, Finn hesitates at the entrance of the library. It's not his usual day to be here, but he couldn't stop thinking about Amber's dismay. She's at the information desk, laughing with a customer. She has such an easy way with people—approaching them with keenness, finding ways to engage. That's all she was trying to do with Finn, and he pushed her away. She stacks books, writes a note and tucks it into the pages of the top one. She responds to a plea for assistance from an elderly gentleman who looks flummoxed by the computer.

Finn waits for his turn. Amber's smile falters momentarily when she notices him, and she blushes. "Hello, can I help?"

"I wanted to apologize for being so rude the other day." He delves into his rucksack and pulls out a small posy of flowers. "I bought you these."

"Oh, that's so sweet. You didn't have to."

"I know, but ..."

She lifts the flowers to her nose. "They're gorgeous, thank you."

They soak up the awkwardness and curious glances from people around them. Neither knows how to extract themselves.

"I should find some water for these," Amber says.

"I just came in for that," Finn says at the same time.

When Finn goes to the library now, it's to see Amber. He doesn't realize it at first, but one restless night, his eyes snap open and he sees Amber's face in the shadows rather than Lexi's. *No, no, stop it.* He's not cut out for relationships. Lexi proved that—Lexi, and Claire who came before her. Claire who sat him down one day and told him she loved someone else.

Yet, each Tuesday he heads for the library once he's finished work and looks forward to seeing Amber's eyes light up in a smile he hopes is just for him. Well, each Tuesday, and also each Friday now—because a week is too long. Occasionally, she'll have a day off, and those afternoons are futile and unsatisfying.

"Anything interesting?" Amber asks, one day, sitting opposite and leaning forward to read upside down.

"No, same old crap." He folds the paper and pushes it aside.

"You really *should* try a book, you know. We've got one or two hanging around."

His cheeks color as he remembers the previous conversation about books. He shakes his head. "I'm not much of a reader."

"Why don't I pick one out for you? *Not* a thriller, something more thought-provoking. No pressure though. I won't be upset if you don't finish it." She pats the table and stands without letting him reply. "Wait here."

She skips across to the shelves, her skirt swishing against her hips, her calves shapely and her hair falling down her back.

Stop. It!

Finn stares at the newspaper, at the large bold headline about impending recession.

Amber returns with a slim book with a black kitten illustration on the cover. "This is one of my favorites." She sets it on the table between them. "It's about a man who makes a deal with the devil. And it's short. I'd love for you to give it a go."

He turns the book over, reading the description. "Okay. I'll do my best."

Despite being a naturally slow reader, he races through the book, eager to impress Amber. He sits in the garden while the sun lasts, or beneath the standard lamp in the living room, with a glass of whiskey in his hand.

"Have you read it?" Amber pounces on him as he walks through the door.

"Yes. And enjoyed it. I've never read a translated novel before. I have a few questions—" He stops as Amber checks her watch and frowns.

"Oh, I'm so sorry, I've got to go. I've got a meeting." She makes no move. She glances at her hands and blushes. "I'm not working tomorrow, perhaps we could meet for coffee and discuss it then? If you want to. Only if you ..."

Finn inhales, his heart rate accelerating. "I'd like that."

The next day, they drink Americanos and talk animatedly about the book Finn's just read, and about others which Amber may persuade him to try. When they stand to leave, Finn asks her out to lunch on Saturday. And after their lunch together, one or other suggests dinner one evening. Ultimately, books are only a small part of their conversation as they broaden into other topics.

Amber continues to recommend books, and Finn reads them beneath the standard lamp with a glass of whiskey.

And this is how Finn falls in love again.

CHAPTER THIRTEEN

LEXI

Your feet slide along the road, scrubbing against the sticky tarmac. The soft squeak of your rubber soles is the only noise. Your hand runs along dry-stone walls and smooth-rendered houses; along the weeds growing in people's gardens, and when you reach the park, along the rusted railings. The vibration numbs your fingers.

It's strange, isn't it, that you should feel numbness, or that when you stub your toe against the curb you feel pain? Surely those things should be beyond your reach.

This park—just a large square of grass with play equipment in one corner and handmade picnic benches in another—is where you spent your teenage years. The early ones ogling older boys playing football, desperate for their attention; the later ones drinking WKD Blue and listening to music late into the night. Recollections of friends linger—their laughter and chatter, their shadows lazing around on the grass.

You've stopped looking for real people, finally acknowledging the pointlessness. You've stopped bracing as you walk around corners or listening for voices. You think of people in the past, as memories, as ghosts who once haunted these streets. Exhaustion makes you compliant and docile. No one here? Yeah, whatever; perhaps they never were.

The heat is aggressive; your skin is on fire. Beads of sweat run down your neck, between your shoulder blades. Yet when you touch your arm, it's cold.

From the park gates, you should be able to see the river and the roofs of houses as they roll down the hill. But the fog has obliterated them. Watch long enough and you'll see it slinking closer.

You jolt and look away with a sense of confusion. Where are you? Oh, the park.

Josh.

Who?

Your first love. The guy who broke your heart.

Isn't it funny how your most recent memories are inaccessible—the argument with Finn, the woman with the balloons in the pub—but Josh, oh yes, he's right there when you'd prefer him not to be.

You were twenty-one; he was in his final year at uni. You worked in the coffee shop he frequented, setting up his laptop each day to write his dissertation. Being in his final year should have been all the warning you needed—he was on the cusp of being free. But you were smitten; you thought you were enough for him. He made you laugh, which with your parents' accident still fresh and raw was commendable. You sat on this very spot as he handed you a plastic Champagne flute of cheap sparkling wine the day after he graduated.

"I'll be going home too," he said, as the bubbles danced in his glass.

"Going? But ..."

"My dad's found me a job with his firm. It's an amazing opportunity."

"I thought you'd be staying here."

"A good salary, great prospects, one of the leading solicitor's firms in Nottingham."

"I thought we'd have more time."

He put his glass down and twisted around to sit in front of you. "Come with me."

If you'd said yes, you wouldn't be here, wherever here is. You'd be so very far away, and so very happy. But you looked out at the deep blue river, and the rolling hills, and recalled playing Frisbee with your dad after school. And you looked at Josh and shook your head.

"I can't."

"It would be a fresh start.

"I can't." So much had changed so quickly. Some people might have needed to flee, to start over; but it was too big an idea for you, too soon, too far away.

A stone, flat and sharp, digs into your palm. You hold it between your forefinger and thumb, flip it into the air and catch it on the back of your hand—a neat party trick. Josh was so excited. He thought he was presenting you with this great gift and his face, when he realized you wouldn't change your mind, crumpled.

You throw the flat, sharp stone but don't see where it lands. Is he still in Nottingham, you wonder, rising through the ranks of the legal profession?

You scratch another stone from the parched soil, the dust catching under your fingernails.

"This one's for Josh," you shout, lobbing it as far as possible.

Then another, shuffling across the grass in search of the perfect size and weight, aiming this time for the old house which shares the boundary with the park, hoping to smash one of the large windows.

"This one's for being so stupid and not going with him!"

It doesn't reach the house. It settles among the leaves of the bountiful beech tree and stays there—your regret—cossetted by the branches.

That word again: regret. Is that all life is, a series of grievances until it's too late to care?

Where does Finn fit, in this quagmire of self-pity? The man who appeared out of nowhere and loved you, and supported you, and trapped you, who was perfect for then but maybe not for now, if you could only get your thoughts in order and stop being so scared of the future? He's the sharpest stone of all, and yet you can't throw him away.

The swings are rusted, and creak when you squeeze your hips between the chains and push yourself back and forth. Your feet leave the ground and the air brushes against your skin. After the stillness of the air for so long, this breeze you create is blissful. You grasp the chain, thrusting forward and leaning back, climbing higher and higher.

"I'm here," you yell into the air. "Come and get me. I'm. Right. Here!"

There's a point, when you're almost level with the top bar, when the chain slackens and for a moment you're suspended, flying.

You could jump. Over the fence and down onto the road. *Should* jump.

Should do something.

You grip tighter, knuckles whitening. With the idea circling in your head, you're scared you'll let go and crash to the rubber matting. You scuff your feet against the ground, lurching to a rapid halt and wrenching your shoulder. You feel the pain. You *feel* it. Your euphoria decreases. Sadness and nostalgia settle like soft snow.

The heat curls around the metal frame; the tarmac melts. Swaddled by the warmth, you sit on the grass and gaze hopelessly at the encroaching fog. It's taken all the views you know so well. From this park, you ought to see for miles. You lie and stare instead at the unhindered clear sky, then close your eyes.

Then sit suddenly. A noise. Wasn't it? Music, a piano maybe, or a radio. Not loud enough to hear properly. And, you realize with a disheartened sigh, not really there at all.

It's getting to you, the isolation. If this really is an afterlife, it's a pretty appalling one. Where are the angels? Where are your parents welcoming you back to them? Is everyone who ever died stuck in their own empty world?

Stop. Too many questions.

The music is still rising into the air. Light and cheery, it draws you towards the concrete steps which lead from the park down to the road. It's coming from the house directly ahead in the shadow of a majestic beech tree. The windows are alive as the reflection of the branches appear to sway, the leaves a jumble of green and brown. Nothing's moving, of course, without a breeze, but your bobbing and weaving gives that effect. You move closer.

In the kitchen window, you see yourself superimposed onto the room—your torso seems to emerge from the sink. How tired you look, how jaded and hopeless.

Movement diverts you. From further into the room, a woman has entered, looking out but not at you. Your reflected features almost interwoven with hers. Her blonde hair with your brown, her plump cheeks with your angular and hollow ones.

Someone else is here. Someone else trapped like you? You wave, shout, bang on the window. Oh, so familiar.

All this time, you've been wrong. You're still alive, and there are others here, just as bewildered as you.

But this woman doesn't seem scared or confused. She's gathering dishes, filling the sink, squirting washing-up liquid into the water—all the normal things you'd be doing if you were at home right now. In an instant, she's gone.

"No! Don't go. Come back!"

It's just you again. You place your forehead on the glass, scanning the room and the place where she was just a moment ago. The barren room, with a sheen of dust and abandonment. You refocus your gaze and see yourself again; you see the desolation etched into your face. And the tears rolling down your cheeks.

CHAPTER FOURTEEN

FINN

It's been two years since Lexi went.

When the longest day comes around again, Finn locks himself away and drinks whiskey and cider, and keeps the curtains closed against the sunshine and prying eyes.

No eyes actually pry anymore, but it's peculiar how the sensation never truly leaves.

Mourning. Is that the right word? The act of remembering those who are lost to us, and of acknowledging the void left behind. Despite the space being slowly occupied by Amber, Lexi remains seared into his head—a shroud covering him, a vestige of his past life. What power she had over him, to still intrude this way.

Does Amber mean less to him than Lexi did? Will she always be second? The notion catches him, makes him choke on his cider.

No, he loves her. He's sure of it. But the guilt he has when he thinks of Lexi keeps her rigidly fixed in his life.

He pours another drink and his finger hovers over the red DECLINE button on another of Amber's calls. Her picture flashes up with each attempt to contact him. It's a photo taken on a recent day trip to the zoo—Amber petting a fluffy goat in a small enclosure, trying to convince Finn to feed the animal. She's looking directly into the camera, laughing, beckoning him closer. At the time, he imagined her crouching beside a child, the way the parents around them were, explaining how they had to be very gentle.

His heart missed a beat when he realized the child he was imagining would be *their* child—his and Amber's. Where had *that* idea come from? He'd reached his forties without ever considering having kids. Not with Lexi, or Claire. But here he was, picturing the family they could become.

That first year was a swamp from which he never thought he'd escape. He saw himself withered and decaying, the male equivalent of Miss Haversham. Yet, with one impulsive detour to the library, his life had changed dramatically.

Finn dismisses Amber's concern, the next day. "I needed time."

"I didn't think ... You never mention her, I didn't think she was important anymore." She chews her thumbnail; she avoids his eye.

Important? Define important. "She's not, not in the way you're implying. When she went, it was abrupt. I struggled."

"Your breakdown?"

"It wasn't a ..." He stops and frowns. Amber moved to the town several months after the gossip had reduced to a background hum, a lingering echo which became distorted with every reiteration. They're still at it, it seems, these busybodies, blathering on about things they don't understand. His fist tightens and Amber watches the veins in his arms bulge.

"Finn?"

"Who told you?"

"Jon, at work."

His eyes narrow at the idea of the two of them tucked away in a corner, heads together, while *Jon* relayed the salacious details, *Jon* who knows nothing other than what's he's picked up and twisted around. Was he trying to dissuade her from seeing Finn, to steal her for himself? Did they laugh at him when he walked into the library and made a beeline for her?

Amber sits beside Finn and takes his hand in both of hers. "Don't be like this. He was just concerned about me. He didn't want me to get in too deep without understanding what had happened. I was wrong to listen. I should have waited for you to tell me what you wanted me to know." She's choosing her words meticulously, pausing to assess the impact of each one.

"No one ever called it a breakdown to my face. Is that what they think?"

"Jon didn't either," she says quickly. "That's my word. I kind of guessed, from the things you've said, and the way the anniversary affected you."

"What must you think of me?"

She shuffles closer and rests her head on his shoulder. "No less than I ever have. She was a big part of your life, and a big part of who you are today. It was a difficult time. We all deal with these things in our own way."

Finn takes a deep breath and holds it within him. "Her aunt made a big deal of it, and the police made an appeal—it made the national papers. It was surreal. It snowballed. Everyone had an opinion. Vultures." He wraps his arms around himself, folding in and protecting himself against the voices which threaten to resurface.

"She never contacted you? She was just gone?"

He nods. "The police have left the case open, so it's never really gone away. I haven't spoken to them or her aunt for a long time."

Amber sits back and considers him carefully, so much whirring around her head. "What were they saying?"

"Sorry?"

"You said 'everyone had an opinion'—what were they saying?"

He smiles grimly. "That I'd chased her off, beaten her so badly she had no choice but to flee, that I had a secret past, that ..." He shrugs. "You name it. People aren't discrete when they want you to hear them." He stands before she has time to formulate another question. "I'm putting the kettle on."

While the kettle boils, Finn stands at the back door and breathes the scent of damp grass. He hardly goes out there anymore—the whim of gardening passed quickly. He suspects it would have for Lexi, too. It's overrun with weeds and brambles; the vegetable patch is indistinguishable from the unkempt lawn. Sometimes, he catches the old bloke from next door glancing over the fence and shaking his head at the chaos.

Amber stands behind him and slips her arms around his waist, her cheek resting against his muscular back.

"Move in with me," he says impulsively, turning and scooping her into his arms, lifting her from the floor as she squeals.

"What?"

"You heard. We should live together. I love you. I want to be with you."

She wriggles free, landing with a bump. "Here?" She glances around at the ghost of Lexi, at the memories preserved in the walls.

Caught in the moment, he forgets himself. "No, somewhere completely new."

How things change. How *he's* changed. For a time, he thought he was lost forever, like Lexi; and here he is, moving into a new place with Amber.

Finn pauses with the last of the boxes taped and labelled and listens to the hum of Amber vacuuming upstairs. At the back door, he considers the garden. He tidied while he was selling, but the new owner will have a big job ahead. He stiffens at the idea of new people in here, wandering these rooms, mirroring his and Lexi's footsteps. A lump forms in his throat, a panicky sensation. He takes a breath, and another, until his heart rate slows to normal.

The black cat slinks towards the house, rubbing against the brambles. Finn never worked out whose cat it is—it seems to wander around as if it owns all the houses in the street, and sometimes it's not seen for several days. It digs at the earth, and Finn rushes out to shoo it away. Not that it matters anymore. It clambers up the wall and sits on top with a defiant, bored yawn. Bright green eyes flash from the black fur and remind him of the book Amber got him to read once.

On their first night in the new house, they eat pizza from the box because they can't locate the plates. Brown cardboard boxes are piled high around them, with a small space cleared so they can at least sit on the sofa rather than the floor.

"Are you happy?" Amber asks.

She always asks, always checks, cajoling him into emotion. Granted, he has the face of a middle-aged man—softening around the jowls, greying at the temples—a face which settles readily into a frown. What does Amber, ten years younger, see in him? How can *she* be happy, he wonders?

"Of course I am. I'm with you."

The new house overlooks the river, on the north side of town, on the side of a hill. It was Amber's choice. Her eyes lit up when she saw the view from the front rooms—the living room downstairs and the master bedroom above. She could hardly tear herself away to talk to the estate agent, drifting back to the window, paying nominal attention.

After living alone, it seems to Finn he has to climb over Amber to get anywhere, although the house is larger than his previous one, with a fourth bedroom and separate dining room. The boxes don't help, he concedes, piled up in their allocated rooms. It'll take weeks to sort themselves out.

"Nonsense," Amber says, staring at the river and the hills beyond, lost in the deep blue and rich greens. "We'll get cracking in the morning and have it done by Friday. We could invite some friends round, have a small housewarming."

Finn tries to contain his reluctance. "I don't have friends to invite."

"What about the blokes down the pub? And your work colleagues?"

"They're not *friends*. We don't socialize." She must know this about him by now.

"Not even at Christmas—the office party?"

"They do something—a meal, or … I don't go."

"Oh, Finn." She laughs lightly, but she studies him and takes a bite of her pizza. When she's finished, and Finn expects her to say something more, she takes another.

"I don't mind a party, if you want one."

She shakes her head. "Maybe we'll do something later on. It doesn't matter."

Over the next few days, Amber unpacks and organizes, while Finn is given specific tasks. When he's completed one thing, he's handed another—small, manageable chunks. From one box, Amber uncovers a photo album, with the protective film curling at the edges. Beneath it are two more. She shifts from kneeling to sitting, her legs stretched out and crossed at the ankles. She lays her palm on the cover as if absorbing the memories held inside.

"Actual albums? A bit old-fashioned, aren't they? Shouldn't you be saving your snaps on a cloud or something?"

"I like the smell, and the sound of the plastic peeling away from itself." She opens it and turns the stiff pages. Sepia photos nestle alongside the vivid hue of the '80s. "When I was little, my gran would sit with me and tell me the stories behind the pictures." She pauses at a bride and groom standing on the steps of a church with confetti falling upon them. Several guests are milling around; a couple are looking towards the photographer. "That's her—my gran—at my parents' wedding. And"— she turns the page in anticipation—"with me a couple of years later." She strokes the photo of an older woman holding a tiny sleeping baby.

Page after page, she smiles at each photo, touches the faces of people no longer with her, chuckling at her own antics. She closes the book wistfully and sets it aside.

"Where's your stuff?" she asks, peeking inside the next box. Finn points. "No, that's the kitchen stuff, and that's your work stuff. I meant personal things—pictures, keepsakes …"

"I threw a lot of things away. This is a fresh start. I wanted a clean slate."

"What about your red chair, and the lamp? I haven't seen them." He shrugs. "Gone."

"Ah. They were her things."

"Just *things*. Not important." He crouches in front of her. "You're important now. Just you." He pulls her into a hug, resting his chin on her shoulder and closing his eyes to prevent Lexi seeping in.

CHAPTER FIFTEEN

LEXI

Maybe you walked here, maybe you're learning how this place works and imagined yourself here and made it happen, but you're standing in front of the 1970s house with its floor-length windows and the lawns in front where you used to live. It's where you took your first steps and learnt to ride a bike; where you made dens in the back garden and played hide-and-seek with your friends. It's where you were happy.

Before you realize it, you're entering and standing in the hall. You're eight again, home from school, jumper dragging on the floor, shoes and socks muddy after playing out at lunch time. The aroma of cheese-on-toast wafts from the kitchen. Mum sings along to an old song playing on the radio. Any moment now, she'll realize you're here. She'll turn with a smile and her arms held out for a hug.

Any moment.

This moment.

The enduring heat returns, pulling you from the fantasy and back to this deserted house.

In the kitchen, you turn on the tap—first, bathing your wrists in the flow and wallowing in its fleeting relief, then hunting for a glass to fill. You gulp, relishing the cool trickle down your throat. Filling and refilling. You weren't thirsty, but now you can't stop.

Through the open back door, you watch laundry drooping on the line and the stealthy fog gobbling the roofs of houses on the adjacent hill.

It's a cluttered room, full of a life on hiatus. Takeaway menus are stuck to the fridge with magnets from Exeter Cathedral and Paignton Zoo. Last night's dishes have been dumped in the sink, waiting to be transferred to the dishwasher. A dog's water bowl but no dog. A jumble of shoes kicked into the corner.

Messy, chaotic, busy—a family rushing around and having fun. You rifle through opened and discarded envelopes on the side—Jess lives here, with her husband Terry F and daughter Miss H.

Upstairs, you peek into the spare room and the master bedroom, inexplicably expecting your dad's shoes to be lined up under the bed and your mum's perfume to be lingering as though she's just spritzed it. You brace yourself for your own room, your *old* room. Miss H's room. No, not that room yet—you're not ready.

At the bathroom door, the sight of the shower is seductive, the idea of plunging yourself beneath cold water, of starting afresh. You strip before you have chance to question if it's a step too far. Breaking into someone's house and disrobing—normal or not?

Either way, you turn on the shower and let the cold water wash the longest day from your body. You angle your head, so the stream runs through your hair. You use lavender soap from the rack, lathering it into opulent suds which soothe you as you inhale the scent. The reprieve from the sweltering heat is blissful.

You leave your sweat-sticky clothes on the bathroom floor and search for clean things. Jess and Terry's bedroom is sleek and modern—her clothes are too neutral and tailored, reminiscent of the outfits you wear to work and hate. Miss H's bedroom is white, but it used to be lilac. The walls used to have Maroon 5 and Avril Lavigne posters taped up wherever there was space, but Miss H has art in black frames. Some of the pictures are signed by her.

This room, these walls. The first space you could call your own; the first door you could slam; the first place you could stamp your personality onto.

The wardrobe is full of cropped t-shirts and wide trousers—stuff you used to wear only a few years ago. It's funny how fashion is never really new, isn't it? You rifle through and find a dress—red with large white daisies across the skirt. It slides over your hips and the fabric swishes when you move.

And then you stop moving and swishing, and the weight of the day crashes down on you again.

Nothing's changing. Nothing's happening. The fog is crawling, creeping, sneaking ever closer—pausing, it seems, when you stand and stare at it, like the games of 'Statues' you used to play with ... you know, that friend, the carrot-cake woman ... Her name escapes you, just like earlier when you couldn't remember ... someone else.

Your memories are dissolving, aren't they? Leaving gaps as though these things, these people, never existed. You barely grasp the things that are missing, you're just aware. You list people: Mila, Phoebe, Finn.

Always Finn.

Oh, Finn.

A breeze rushes into the room. You jolt. A door slams and you jump to attention.

Footsteps on the stairs, moving across the landing. Stomp, stomp.

You shouldn't be here, in someone else's house. With wet hair, wearing Miss H's dress, like a modern-day Goldilocks—how mortifying it'll be to be caught out. You should hide, but there's nowhere to go. Under the bed. In the wardrobe. You dither, side-stepping, but ultimately remaining exactly where you are.

The door bursts open. You brace yourself, defiantly. Miss H's smile falters. Startled, pale, she points at you.

"That's my ..." She fumbles for something on the chest of drawers behind her. Her fingers find a chunky wooden bracelet which she throws at you.

And.

Nothing.

Of course, nothing.

The bracelet doesn't hit you or crash to the ground. It's just gone. Miss H is absorbed into the walls. Her shock turns to disbelief as she fades. You watch the space left behind, shivering in a breeze no longer blowing.

One of you was real. Which one?

Perhaps both of you, both stuck in a crack between time. This place and the other one crashing together for a split second. It means, they're still there. It means—

Each turn you take brings you back to the same thought.

You run. Down the stairs and out into the blistering heat. You run. To the end of the road, where the junction takes you down the hill or up the hill. But you don't know which way to turn. Neither will take you where you want to go.

"I'm not dead!"

Your voice is an aberration sending shards of noise into the fissure between here and there. It bounces off the abandoned houses and down into the valley, stopping when it hits the fog. You expect an echo, but it doesn't come. The fog catches it and holds it.

You slump down in the middle of someone's garden, allowing yourself once more to sink into this nonsensical world, allowing your body to grow heavy, to grow roots, to never leave.

Pink gravel frames the lawn—a peculiar color choice, stealing attention from the roses and foxgloves. The stones are too small and irregular to stack, but you find yourself idly gathering them into piles, and the piles form the shape of an L, then an E on the lawn. You gather more and make the letters larger, the thickness of your arm—no, bigger than that. The X and I snake onto the pavement when you run out of room.

"Lexi."

It doesn't sound right. How long since you've heard your name spoken aloud?

Finn said it many times last night—acid with annoyance or muttering it under his breath. He was cross with you; no, worse, furious. Was it something specific or another symptom of a relationship failing? Last night, and so long ago. How are you supposed to remember something so far away and implicit? You close your eyes and picture the restaurant. Or maybe *a* restaurant on an entirely different night. Mondays aren't for eating out. Why were you out last night?

"Alexandra," you say. The name on your birth certificate, your passport, countless letters from your parents' solicitors. The name you hated from the moment your tongue stumbled over all the syllables and couldn't form the sounds and you wrote the letters in the wrong order. The name of a saint or an empress, not a child with red chubby cheeks and a keenness for muddy puddles.

Only your mother called you Alexandra, and only when she was very, very cross. Daddy never did. He called you Beach. In front of your friends. Which means you had to explain: Alexandra, shortened to Sandy, lengthened to Sandy Beach, shortened to … "Ah, Beach," they'd say, with an expression of slight perplexity.

You throw the remainder of the stones towards the house. A couple hit the window with a satisfying *chink*. Stray ones hit the bonnet of their car and leave little dinks in the paintwork.

CHAPTER SIXTEEN

FINN

In a small room, with a handful of guests, Finn marries Amber. It's a simple ceremony; over in the blink of an eye.

He knows it's not the day she pictured or deserved, but they both appreciated he wouldn't have handled a larger affair. Even this, among family and a few close friends, is testing. His voice shakes throughout the vows; Amber squeezes his hand reassuringly, reminding him to focus solely on her. His speech is short but emotive.

The bride is radiant, eleven weeks pregnant. Their secret. Although by the end of the day people will be wondering. Amber takes the tiniest of sips during the toasts, and refuses offers of another drink as she makes her way around the guests. She says: *I've just had one, thank you* and *Are you trying to get me tipsy?* even though she's the most sober person there.

Finn draws back and watches his new wife mingle with her friends, and pose for photos, and show off her ring. *His wife.* It's all so surreal. When she catches his eye, he smiles and thinks himself unbelievably lucky.

On his side, the guest list is frugal. Most of his friends have dropped away over the past five years. His colleagues from work make an appearance—arriving together and departing after an hour, with polite murmurs of congratulation.

He wondered if he should invite Phoebe, but in the end, he simply informed her he was getting married. She needed to know. He wanted to write, but Amber insisted he should call.

Phoebe didn't say anything for a long time. "I see." Clipped, curt.

"I didn't want you hearing it from someone else."

"I see."

"It's been five years. Don't you think it's time—?"

"Thank you for letting me know." And she hung up.

Finn's father and sister occupy one corner, pushing two tables together to make room for her kids and husband, Steve. The two girls dance and play tag around adult legs while their teenage brother plays on his phone. They don't get together often. The last time Finn saw his nieces, they were toddlers and his mother—still alive and not yet beset with the ailment that took her—was running around after them. His father only met Amber for the first time a couple of months ago.

Amber's with them, chatting easily as if she's known them forever. He should be beside her, joining in with the celebrations and accepting the good wishes people are bestowing, but he's at the bar in the opposite corner. A halo of space has formed around him. He orders a pint and stares at the frothy white head.

"So, you finally got hitched, mate. Congrats." Dean appears from nowhere and slaps him on the back.

Dean, who stopped caring after a year of constant support. Dean, who abandoned him like Lexi did. Dean, who Finn doesn't remember inviting. Amber must have searched through the contacts on his phone. Would she *do* that?

Dean, who orders a Coke oblivious to the hostility. "Driving," he explains. "You look like you've seen a ghost."

"I wasn't expecting to see you here."

Dean laughs. "Ah, right. Amber knows my missus, and I thought, what the heck, it's been a while. Thought it would be good to catch up." He glances around. "Nat's over there, if you want to say hello." He sips his drink and considers Finn carefully. "Maybe not, eh? She was never your favorite person. Funny, though, us knowing Amber *and*—"

Finn tenses, hunching further over his pint. "So, what's new with you?"

"I'm a math teacher now. Went back to uni and retrained. And I'm back playing a bit of rugby." He chuckles. "Got myself into a team of old codgers. I'm only forty-four—I don't feel old enough, but apparently, I am. It's a good laugh, and we're not bad. Fifth in the league. You should come and have a go, rediscover the old Finn."

"The old Finn?"

"Well, yeah. The one before Lexi turned you soft, the up-for-anything Finn."

Lexi's name, out in the open, unnerves him. He glances at Amber in case she overheard. He looks towards the door as if Lexi will walk in and demand to know what the hell is going on. He frowns. It's his wedding day—he shouldn't be thinking about *her*.

What the fuck is Dean doing here anyway? His lip curls into a snarl. "And you're *up for anything* these days, are you? Father of two, math teacher. Yeah, right."

"Aw, come on, mate—I didn't mean it like that." Dean grins nervously. "You should be above my stupid banter, especially today."

"Things change, that's all I'm saying."

The space between them expands although neither has moved. They drink with tentative animosity while music thuds from the side of the bar and several people are heading for the dancefloor. Dean finishes his Coke and slams the glass onto the bar.

"I'd better get back to Nat. I'll see you around sometime, yeah?" He hovers for a second, allowing Finn time to say something else, then walks back to his wife, wrapping his arms around her waist and resting his chin on her shoulder. He whispers in her ear, and they both glance across to Finn.

Friends are a weird phenomenon. Finn understands team-mates—the entrenched bond which occurs when you're striving for a common goal—and work colleagues for the same reason, to some extent. And even the regular faces at the pub who'll exchange comments about the England line-up and offer to buy another round. But he's never felt the inclination to share his worries and fears, his joys, his life, with anyone. Glancing across the room to Amber, hugging her parents and dragging them onto the dancefloor, he understands relationships even less—but it's too late to ponder how two individuals can coexist over the course of years and decades without traveling different paths. It's too late to contemplate if this was a mistake.

No, of course it isn't. He loves Amber.

He loved Lexi, and she went.

He loved Claire, and she did too.

As the pint glasses gather around him and the room seems softer than it did, Amber takes his hand and coerces him to dance with her. He follows her to the middle of the room and people pull back to create space for them. He wraps his arms around her waist, and she rests her head on his chest. He inhales the flowery scent of her perfume, light and airy.

"What have you been doing over there all by yourself?"

"You look so beautiful, I wanted to watch you."

"It's your wedding too—you don't seem to be having fun."

"I am, I promise. Are you happy?"

"Very," she murmurs sleepily, pulling herself closer so the small baby bump is nestled between them.

The resulting photo—taken by a friend who appeared beside them at the perfect moment—is her favorite. It'll take pride of place on their mantelpiece for many years.

***

Six months after the wedding, Finn watches his baby being born. He cries. The baby cries. Their tears mingle as Finn holds his son for the first time, and the baby gazes into his eyes. Amber, slick with sweat and fatigue, is beautiful. He soothes the baby while she sleeps and his whole life before this moment dissolves. None of it matters. Any second without this child in it is no longer relevant.

They name him George, and he quickly becomes Georgie. He's the image of Amber, with pouting lips and strawberry blond hair, while Amber says he's got Finn's piercing eyes. They are complete, the three of them together. When they put him in his crib at night, they curl up together on the bed and Amber falls asleep gazing at their beautiful child. Finn doesn't sleep. He watches them both in wonderment.

Finn's preference would be to continue working three days a week and spend the rest of the time with Georgie and Amber, but when Bea retires, he's offered her two days on top of his own, so now he works full-time. With a new family, he could hardly say no. Husband, father, provider. What man wouldn't step up when required?

He gets in early, around seven most days—leaving when Amber is lying in bed feeding Georgie—so he can continue to finish at half-past three. He gets a lot done in the hour and a half before anyone else arrives. He relishes the peace and the steady grumble of commuter traffic pouring down Fore Street.

On the first warm day of spring, when Georgie's about four weeks old, Amber is waiting on the bench outside Finn's office, rocking the pram to pacify him. He likes to keep moving and becomes unsettled when the motion ceases.

"What are you doing here?" Finn asks, slightly more abruptly than he intended.

"We were shopping. I thought it would be nice to have a coffee together before going home."

"Oh." He glances up and down the long street of shops. He still likes to walk to the park after work, strolling home the long way round. It breaks up the day; it calms him.

"We don't *have* to," she says defensively. "I thought it would be *nice.*"

"Of course it would be nice, it's a lovely idea. I'm sorry." He leans forward to kiss her cheek and peer into the pram. He rests his hand lightly on the blanket, feeling the warmth of the sleeping child.

They head down to their favorite coffee shop, with its small tables on either side of the entrance and a concrete canopy above. Amber parks the pram and Finn goes in to order, engrossing himself with the menu on the wall to avoid eye contact with anyone he might recognize. While the coffees are being made, he adds a couple of muffins to the tray. Amber will like that.

She's talking to someone when he takes their snack outside. A woman with a school-uniformed child beside her and a buggy of her own. They're both laughing and turn when Finn approaches. And that's when he realizes who the woman is. Too late to turn around; too late to hide inside until she's gone. "Finn, this is Vanessa. She was in my ante-natal class. Van, this is my husband, Finn."

They're both flustered while Amber continues her introduction, unaware of the stiffness surrounding her.

"Hello Finn. It's been a long time." Vanessa doesn't smile.

"Hello." His voice cracks.

"You know each other?" Amber says with enthusiasm. Finn can tell she's bowling ahead of herself, with ideas for dinner parties and barbeques, and day trips with the kids.

He shakes his head. "Not really. A long time ago."

Vanessa opens her mouth, but nothing comes out. She nods in accord and rests her hand on her daughter's shoulder. She turns to Amber. "We should be going. We'll have to grab a coffee sometime." Her eyes dart to Finn before smiling warmly at Amber and maneuvering the buggy around the tables and up the road.

Finn charts her progress along the pavement until she's absorbed by the glut of schoolkids idling home. His coffee is flavorless. He pushes the muffin aside.

"What's wrong?"

"Nothing. Long day, that's all."

How quickly do people move on and forget? Does Vanessa wake each morning thinking of her friend who left without a word, or is she only reminded when things happen such as seeing Finn again after so long?

Married with a child: would she have expected it of him? Her expression held no emotion when she looked at him, no surprise or concern. Perhaps she was simply unsure how much Amber knows. Even so, it's disconcerting when the past and present collide.

CHAPTER SEVENTEEN

LEXI

Oxygen is depleting. Each inhalation garners less benefit and requires more effort. Limbs are awkward and encumbered; the relentless heat hampers every movement.

You're retracing your steps, following the finite paths and roads which all lead back to Fore Street, if you walk them long enough. You're growing increasingly familiar with every decrepit fence and overgrown bramble, passing small piles of stones you don't recall making.

Outside the old hospital, you say, "That's where I fell off my bike and broke my arm," as though someone's close enough to hear.

In the carpark behind the Co-op: "That's where Dad caught me drinking Strongbow after my last GCSE exam."

And, in Tincombe where a rope swing once hung across the stream: "That's where I cried on a friend's shoulder because some boy dumped me."

Which boy? Which friend? You've got to remember, got to keep it all inside you. You are the things you've done, the people you've met, the things you've seen. It all remains and forms the person you grow into.

Is this how it's going to end, turning circles, seeing the same sights over and over until darkness falls? *If* darkness falls.

The watches on your wrist are heavy, time-weighted. The leather straps cut into your skin. You scratch at the buckle of the first, and the knots of the other, but they're tight and unyielding, a reminder.

And oh, *that fog*, continuing its relentless crawl through the streets and plunging over trees nestled in the dells between neighborhoods, enveloping houses and pinching at the brows of hills. For long periods you pretend it's not even there— ignoring it or simply failing to notice it. But when you do, when you stop and watch the town being swallowed, unease creeps from your stomach and lodges in your throat. It seems reluctant to come too close. It's skulking at the end of a road or masking the tall tower at the fire station, but when you walk in that direction it steps backwards, revealing those things. It'll catch up with you eventually, but for now, it's taunting you, playing a game.

And right now, it's settled on a house you know, across the valley. A friend's house. Your friend's house. Which friend? Remember her—it's important you remember.

The last time you were at that house, just a week or so ago, you sat in the garden and drank wine as the sun began to set and the sky turned lilac. You remember the sky. She opened a bottle of wine for you, but her glass remained empty.

Who? Your friend. Remember.

"I'm pregnant," she said with an expression that was a smile and a frown at the same time.

You shrieked together and laughed and jumped up and down with delight and when you paused to sip your wine she burst into tears.

"It's my hormones," she said, dabbing her eyes with the sleeve of her shirt. "I can't help it—the silliest thing, and I'm off."

"But you're happy, aren't you?" You held her hand; she leant her head on your shoulder.

"Of course I am." Tears welled again. "It wasn't planned. None of this"—she waved her hands to encompass the garden and the house, then rested them on her stomach—"was *planned.*" She bent forward and lowered her voice. "It's like I fell into this life by accident. I never saw myself staying here, in the same town I grew up in. Who does that?"

"We did, lots of people did." *Where are the names? Where are the people you used to know? How can they have faded so easily?*

"Because it was easy. Life shouldn't be easy. It should be thrilling and unexpected and adventurous. We should have done so much more."

"We're only thirty, don't write us off yet!"

Your friend gestured at her barely swollen stomach and raised an eyebrow. "I don't think I've got a choice."

You drained your glass and her regret became your own. How many plans you'd had, how many cast aside when you met … Finn, when you met Finn.

That's when it changed. As recently as a few days ago when you questioned your choices and your future. You've been replaying her words in your head, and they could be your own. You swapped traveling for a mortgage, freedom and excitement for a steady wage and weekends watching the local rugby team. It happened so slowly you never questioned it. But the chains tightened, one link at a time.

Your resentment, barely tangible before that evening, drifted to the surface and was given a life of its own.

Now there's no friend, no bump. No one to hug you and tell you everything will be all right or to keep your wine glass topped up.

There are no work colleagues; no regulars at the bus stop. Nobody to open a door for you or to get in your way.

No Aunt Phoebe. No Finn.

The thought wanes as quickly as it appeared, because there's no point dwelling on it. There's not much point in anything at all.

You're standing in the middle of the road and staring at nothing at all. The weeds in the cracks of the pavements are crisp and brown; flowers in gardens are wilting.

There comes a point in isolation when your thoughts cease, when your senses shut down one by one until you're sitting or standing completely dormant. You may be vaguely aware of the things around you—you might find your attention caught by the scratched-away lettering of a road sign or a crooked roof tile or the scrunched-up newspaper left on a bench in the park. And one of those things will be the last thing you see before you turn inwards, leaving no trace of yourself.

All you have is the sound of your slow, methodical breathing on the inert air.

You pluck petals from a rose and let them fall to the floor.

They don't stop falling.

Behind the long row of shops on Fore Street, a church rises into the limitless sky. Instead of passing by, you go inside. It's cool, calm, reverent. Outside seems far away. The hairs on your arm bristle; your breath catches on the air.

It's a strange place to want to be, but perhaps death does that to a person, uncovers their latent religious beliefs.

You echo around the high ceiling, your presence pulsating against the walls and into the carved moldings. The uneven slate floor holds centuries of prayer while fragile bones lie beneath. The wooden pews are smooth from the millions of hands which have brushed over them. The varnish has chipped away or been carved with the names and artless patterns of bored children. You slip into one of them, unsure if you should kneel or bow. Some people make the sign of the cross, don't they? Instinctively, your palms are pressed into the shape of a prayer, and when you realize, you wedge them between your thighs.

"I'm lost."

Your words are a sigh, a murmur, rising into the air.

"Help me. I don't know what to do."

The stained-glass window casts colored beams of sunlight onto the altar. Particles of dust waver and flutter. So, there must be a breeze or a draught from *somewhere*. Or perhaps it's the impact you're still having on the world—your breath on this lifeless air becoming a tsunami.

Hanging on the stone walls are plaques with beautiful dedications to loved ones—souls who would have had no concept of their lives still being acknowledged a century later. Normal people who led ordinary lives, and here you are reading about them.

One brass plate shines brighter than the others—not more recent, just more polished and tended. *Mary Bowen, born 18 Sept 1876, died 27 Sept 1906. In His arms.* You lean forward to trace the engraving with your finger. Poor Mary Bowen. Thirty years old, the same as you. Poor Lexi Peters.

At the back of the nave, hidden by a thick embroidered curtain, are stairs leading to the tower. You hike up worn stone steps, using a rope attached to the wall to steady yourself. At the top, a large bell hangs in the center. On each of the four walls, narrow openings have slatted shutters. When you lightly run your fingers across one, it crashes to the floor sending dust billowing into the air. Sunlight streams through.

In the ceiling is a trapdoor, a rickety ladder set beneath it. You check for stability, press your foot on the floorboards it's standing on, and test the bottom rung. It bows, emits a slight splintering, but it holds. One step, then another—giving each a tentative push before letting your whole weight bear down. At the top, you squeeze through the opening and out onto the flat roof.

It's hot like hell after the frostiness of the church. Sweat trickles from your hairline and you breathe heat into your lungs. You gaze out with such hope and anticipation. On a clear day you'd see towards the moors and out to sea from here; you'd see the spread of the city suburbs across the river. And it would be beautiful.

The fog travels further than you thought. There's no other side. This small piece of town that you're standing in is all that's left.

You knew it, of course, but disappointment rises. What were you expecting? Something. Some glimmer of the world outside, some flash, some life. Even if it were an illusion. Which it would be, wouldn't it? Surely your mind could create something that felt just a little bit real.

You peer over the low turrets. Down and down to the pavement below.

Could you jump from here? Would you land splattered on the flagstones, arms and legs splayed and broken? If you're dead already, it would hardly matter—you can't die twice. You might simply brush yourself off and continue along your way. You might.

Visions of Bill Murray offing himself in *Groundhog Day* loop around your head. In the film, he wakes at the exact same time of the same day and relives it over and over. For you, it *is* the same time of the same endless day. For the character, it's a deliverance—he smiles as he drives over a cliff or jumps in front of a car.

You don't smile.

The centuries-old wall crumbles beneath your fingers and the moss is crisp. A stone dislodges, and you hop backwards. Almost. You *almost* slipped and fell. And you're not ready. In that moment of whatever half-life existence this is, your survival instinct remained intact. You skirt back to the trapdoor and to the ladder, and hurry down to safety.

CHAPTER EIGHTEEN

FINN

This is how time passes.

You fall into the routine of waking and working and spending weekends at the beach or the petting zoo or in soft play centers when it's too wet to be outside. Your house fills with toys and nappies and endless piles of clothes you're too exhausted to put away. You're on an endless treadmill of feeding your child mushed up swede and carrot or concerned about a rash or mopping up and wiping down.

You wake up and go to work, day after day; the weeks turn into months, the seasons change. You plan holidays and dinner parties and where you'll spend Christmas. You save for a new kitchen and swap energy providers and choose schools and panic that every decision is the wrong one.

And everyone around Finn gets older. Apart from Amber, who grows more beautiful. She's nursing their new-born daughter, Isla, on the sofa with her hair falling across her face while Georgie watches cartoons and laughs at the silly jokes.

Family tethers him. Tighter than the straps on Isla's car seat; stronger than the vines winding around Rapunzel's tower in Georgie's favorite fairy tale.

His previous life, his hermit wilderness months, are fragments scattered across the river, drifting on the tide. Occasionally, a residual sense of people staring grips him, squeezes him at the throat until it's hard to speak or swallow, and abates as quickly.

The longest day of the year comes round with increasing speed. He marks the day with a bottle of Jack Daniels, hiding away in his study, wallowing in drunken despondency.

"It's something I have to do," he tells Amber, although he can't say why.

"Maybe it's something you *don't* have to do anymore," she says, flourishing a hand towards his children, his future. "We could go out for the day—have a picnic on the moors?"

"You don't understand."

"Because you never explain it."

The fight escalates—some years more than others. Neither wins. Finn retreats to his study and Amber throws spoons against the wall.

Married life isn't easy. At forty-seven, only ten of his adult years have been spent alone. With Claire and Lexi, he had an element of freedom which the commitment of marriage doesn't allow. Nothing untoward, nothing devious or hurtful, he's simply aware there was an absence of inevitability. Each day with Claire or Lexi he could have chosen to walk away.

With a large mortgage, money is tight. Amber goes back to work when Isla's six months old, and they juggle childcare—passing sleepy children between them and the nursery. Amber frets over the bills. It wasn't like this with Lexi, when he earned almost twice as much and could have progressed through the company to earn even more. He used up all his savings in the year after Lexi went. It seems a waste, looking back.

"I'm sorry," he says, as Amber moves money from one account to another to cover direct debits and the accidental overspend at Christmas.

"We're managing. Everything's fine."

"If I was in my old job—"

"Either we'd never have met, or you'd never see your kids."

Of course they wouldn't have met. The Finn he used to be would never have walked into the library that day. As horrendous as it was, his missing year brought him to this moment, *this* life, with his beloved children and cherished wife. He bends to kiss the top of Amber's head, but winces when he catches sight of her calculations.

"We probably shouldn't have bought this house," she continues. "We should have gone for something smaller and cheaper." Her eyes flicker towards the window. It's nighttime, but the curtains are open so she can see the streetlights and house lights following the rise and fall of the hill. The river is enveloped by the darkness, but it's there.

"But then you wouldn't have had your view."

"Exactly. We both made choices. Now we live with the reality of them. And it's not so bad—we'll figure it out."

***

On Sunday mornings, Finn takes Georgie and Isla to the park so Amber can have a lie-in, although he suspects she does housework in her pajamas and ducks into the shower when she hears them return. Most weeks, they're here long before anyone else, enjoying the whole park to themselves.

They run up and down the slope with a ball or a kite when it's windy, with Finn chasing after them breathlessly. They never tire out, despite the broken nights and early rises.

Georgie likes the swings best and waits patiently to be lifted into the seat. Meanwhile, Isla toddles unsteadily towards anything hazardous. Then Georgie wants to play on the slide, then the climbing frame. Each week he follows his own little sequence around the equipment with Isla following in his wake desperate to do what her brother can.

As spring unfolds and the mornings lighten, more people emerge to encroach on their space, and Finn has to teach Georgie how to share.

"Hi. Finn? Hi."

Finn closes his eyes and composes himself before turning to face Vanessa. Georgie's already playing with her little one, so he has no choice but to smile and say hello.

"They're friends at nursery." Vanessa nods towards them both. Her little girl is showing Georgie a dandelion, and Georgie's considering it carefully. "They're so sweet together, aren't they?"

"Lovely," Finn mumbles, watching Isla in case she should provide him with an excuse to escape.

"You've got your hands full. It's funny—I never had you down as a family man."

His head spins a little. He bites his lip. "Things change."

"Of course." She gazes out across the roofs, over to the river and the lush green valley it carves through. "I had coffee with Amber the other day—did she tell you? She's lovely. You made a good choice. I'm glad you're happy after ... everything."

Lexi. After Lexi. He's winded, punched in the stomach by unanticipated memories. Not here, he doesn't want to think about her here.

"You seem so suited to fatherhood. I'm not sure Lexi wanted children. You—" She stops, wide-eyed and red-faced. She slaps her hand across her mouth. "Oh God, I'm sorry. That was such an insensitive thing to say. I meant ..." She grasps for words before shaking her head. "Ignore me. I'm so sorry."

She reaches for Finn's arm, but he steps away. He has no idea what she meant, or what she thought she meant. But he doesn't want to think about Lexi. She's always lurking, off-setting his happiness with little reminders of herself. He'll walk into a room and smell her perfume, or her favorite song will be on the radio. But she *shouldn't* be in the park where his kids play.

"Daddy, Daddy. Can Isabella and me play over there?"

"No. We have to go." Too sharp, too snappish. He rarely shouts, and Georgie's face crumples. "Another time." He glances around for Isla, avoiding Vanessa's further attempts at an apology. "We have to go home and see Mummy, don't we? She'll be waiting for us."

He wrestles Isla into the pushchair. He takes Georgie's hand and pulls him away from his friend. They both complain all the way home.

Amber greets them at the door, taking coats and shoes, and directing Georgie to the fresh raisin cookies she's made.

"What's wrong? You're clammy." She presses an ice-cold hand against Finn's cheek. "You're burning up. Go and lie down. I'll bring you some water."

The walls tumble around him as he walks up the stairs, while Amber mutters something about chicken pox running through nursery. There's mud on his hands from the park, from carrying Isla after she'd walked through a puddle, but he's too drained to wash them.

Mud.

There was mud the day Lexi ...

He lies on the bed, staring at his hands. Memories fall around him like autumn leaves.

He's with her again. Watching her dig the dry earth, wiping a hand across her sweaty face and leaving a streak of soil. Determined to create her wretched vegetable garden and live off the produce. Finn doubted she had the patience to grow anything. He joked how the plant in the kitchen was just a dried-out husk.

"You could kill a cactus," he laughed.

"Piss off." Her tone wasn't jovial, and he retreated.

Amber comes in with a cold compress and rests it on his head. "I need to check you for spots," she says, lifting his T-shirt and running her hands across his stomach. "Oh, bugger."

He dreams about digging. His hands red raw as the grating wooden handle of his spade rubs blisters into his palms. His arms and back ache; the sun beats down and saps his energy. It's so hot he's melting into the ground. Now it's cooler, nighttime; the silver moonlight shines across the lawn, and the trees are silhouetted by the faint crown of the impending dawn.

The spade disappears and he's using his bare hands, scraping frantically at the ground, mud catching beneath his nails. It's not deep enough. He claws at the ground.

"Finn, Finn, ssssh. It's okay. You're dreaming." Amber switches on her bedside lamp and holds a glass of water to his lips. She rests her palm on his forehead, and he sighs. "You've got a temperature. Here, take these." She helps him swallow paracetamol and lowers him back onto his pillow.

***

The children grow: first up, then away.

One moment they're clinging to Finn, unsteady on their feet, the next they're skipping to school. They're tiny in new uniforms, which are full and straining at the seams in the blink of an eye.

Years slip by, one to the next. Up and away. Scuffed knees give way to arguments over homework; Finn's still building wooden rail tracks while the kids are on games consoles in their rooms. He remembers sleep-deprived nights, and fever-riddled chicken pox—his and theirs afterwards—and infinite games of Snap and Hungry Hungry Hippos, and the way they'd fall asleep in the back seat on long car journeys. One day they happily hold his hand as they walk along the street, the next they pull away and cross their arms. Up. Away.

These snippets aren't tied to a specific moment. They're mosaics, someone else's reality wrapped around him. He should be living in a dark, dark room, in a dark neglected house. He should be peering warily from a window with overgrown bushes hiding him from the road.

He has nightmares he's trapped in that dark house with no way out, with walls which move to squash him as he walks through the long, shadowed hallways. Yet when he wakes, it feels as though *this* is his dream. It takes several minutes of listening to Amber breathing evenly beside him to grasp which side of the dream he's on.

Finn watches TV while Amber crochets. She glances up, smiles at him the way she has for years, and continues with her task. She's making a bag for Isla—they went shopping for the wool together and had lunch afterwards. Amber cherished every moment because it won't be long before Isla will baulk at spending time with her parents. Georgie's already reached that age.

He remembers pushing his own parents away, but he also remembers coming through the other side—the football-and-pint afternoons with his dad, the Sunday roasts his mum loved to cook.

Isla's in her bedroom while Amber slaves over the bag.

"Shouldn't she be helping you? I thought that was the idea."

"Oh, it's okay. I like doing it. Anyway, she's doing homework."

"With that racket?" He can clearly hear every lyric being uttered; he can clearly hear Isla singing along. He moves to stand but Amber rests her hand on his arm.

"You're showing your age, old man," she says with a smile.

She doesn't mean it, but he nods grimly. That's exactly what he is. Too old to be a father of teens. His rugby mates from all those years ago are watching *their* kids getting married. Dean—who in a maddening twist of fate coaches Georgie's team—is a grandfather. And he's tired, dragging himself from bed in the mornings and trudging to work. The evenings don't come fast enough, then it starts all over again the next day. Lexi weighs him down—his head is peppered with her, as if she's tapping him on his shoulder to remind him she's there.

"Hey." Amber's kneeling beside him, her hand squeezing his. "Are you okay? You zoned out for a moment. You were mumbling."

"I'm just tired. I might have an early night."

"It's half-past eight."

He smiles and pats her hand. "You said it, I'm an old man."

"We should book a holiday." She pauses and glances down at their fingers still laced. "Or perhaps you could think about reducing some of your hours?"

"Retire?"

"No, just cut down a bit. Drop a day, see how it goes."

In bed, he doesn't sleep. He listens to the drone of Isla's music, the bustle which occurs when Georgie returns home and dashes to the bathroom for a shower, the theme tunes which announce the end of one show and the start of another. The night is unsettled and muddled. Life is moving too quickly.

CHAPTER NINETEEN

LEXI

A story is not a story without action. A life is not a life without someone to share it with.

No more lingering and hanging around. No more waiting. How much longer do you want to remain in this limbo? Surely doing *something* is better than doing *nothing*.

What would Finn do?

To be honest, you have no idea. He's fading like a dream that was so vivid just a moment ago. A moment, a lifetime. You hold the name in your hand, but you have no idea to whom it belongs. *No, not Finn.* Just an illusion now, a vague notion. There was a man in a bar when you went out with friends. There was an argument. A tall, strong man walking towards you, offering you a drink, A man grabbing you by the wrist and pulling you along.

None of it makes sense anymore. Your memories are not memories; they're stories.

And a story isn't a story without action.

The road you're on is long—the retail park in one direction, Fore Street in the other because all roads lead that way. The fog is hiding both of them. You idly test the door of the next car you come to, because the streets are full of them, taunting you with the prospect of freedom, although you've been ignoring them. Why would you bother when you never learnt to drive? Cars are never your first thought.

But here they are, and why not give it a try. You expect the door to open because if this is a dream or coma-based hallucination, nothing exists beyond your own will and desire. It doesn't open.

The black cat, Luci, sits on the pavement opposite, upright, his tail curled around his body.

"Are you following me?"

He licks a paw with deep concentration and washes behind his ear.

"What am I supposed to do? This?" You try another door. "Probably not this." And another. "Are you here to help, to guide me to ...?"

To where? What comes next?

Luci pauses, paw to its mouth, considering the question and staring with those unblinking emerald eyes.

"Yeah, that's what I thought."

The fourth car opens. The keys are in the ignition.

You swallow. "Okay."

You don't have a plan for this, but with just a moment's pause, you slide into the driver's seat and place both hands on the steering wheel. The leather is hot and burns your hands; you let go quickly.

It's odd being on this side of the car, the *wrong* side. You turn the key for lack of anything else to do. The car splutters and lurches forward. The cat flees. The engine dies.

Stop. Think. You close your eyes and try to picture all the times you've watched other people. Which other people? It doesn't matter anymore, does it? These long-gone people who exist only as movement in your peripheral vision.

Gear in neutral, turn the key, clutch and accelerator balanced. You hop forward again, but the engine comes to life. As it ticks over, you mull the options: head out of town, face the fog, and pray. Or perhaps … not. Perhaps there's a different way, a drastic and permanent way.

You close your eyes, take a deep breath, and press the accelerator to the floor.

The engine roars. Splitting the air. Pulsating through the chassis, up through the steering wheel and your arms and into your stomach.

Tires screech and squeal on the searing hot tarmac.

Houses zoom past. The football ground, the police station, the care home.

The fog recedes, creating a wide avenue.

The park on the left, the church, Victoria Gardens on the right. You gather momentum.

The road rolls to the right, but you steer left. The wall ahead races towards you.

Faster, faster. Smash!

The air bag inflates and pushes you against the headrest. You remain still for a moment, eyes closed, mentally checking each arm and leg, ascertaining pain from your head or your chest. There's no blood, no pain; no change.

"Shit."

You fumble for the door and squeeze yourself out onto the road, scraping your knee on the curb.

"Shit!"

You stare at the car, crumpled and broken, and laugh. Because what else is there to do?

You grab one of the dislodged rocks from the wall and ram it into the car. The metal yields and dents; flecks of paint float into the air. You grab another rock and throw it against the windscreen which shatters but holds itself together. You don't stop; you can't. You punch the precarious glass, and it smashes into tiny pieces, slashing your hand. Blood drips along your arm.

"See." You hold your hands up, tilting your head towards the sky. "Action. Now it's your turn!"

Of course, nothing happens.

Not immediately.

There's a chill against your skin, and a faraway noise you can't decipher. You see flowers in the raised bed flutter, and rain gently patters onto the pavement—individual drops hitting the ground before they spread out and meet. The smell of damp earth rises, and you breathe it in.

Steadily, the street fills with ghosts, with people who look like they don't belong. As they walk along, they become more corporeal, fleshed out, real.

So many people. But none of them have noticed you, or the car half buried by the wall. They walk past it; it almost seems as though they're walking *through* it.

"Hi, hello."

They're steadfastly looking straight ahead, lost in their own worlds.

A bus pulls up to the curb and passengers pour out; an air ambulance speeds towards the hospital and a toddler points with excitement. Traffic lights beep and the green man flashes. So many things all at once.

"Hello, please? Where have you all been?"

You glance at your watches—it's been so long and yet no time at all. The hands remain unmoving. Surely, they should be ticking, seconds and minutes and hours passing again. And there he is. Finn. A man you know so intimately but don't know at all. The man who is vanishing from your memories, right here in front of you. He's older, wearier, trudging nonchalantly through the rain, weighed down by the large bag he's carrying on his shoulder.

"Finn." Not a real sound, a tiny squeak. "Finn."

His eyes are on the pavement, looking down, avoiding you, avoiding everyone.

You walk backwards, facing him, trying to remain in sight. And eventually he looks up, looks at you, stares hard for a moment—his expression morphing into something hideous and repellent, hardening into fear or shock or disbelief. He stops suddenly, and the young mother following behind maneuvers to avoid catching his ankles with her pram. In the middle of the pavement, he closes his eyes, mouthing *one, two, three*.

When he opens them, he begins to fade. Everyone does.

"No, wait." You reach for him. "Take me with you."

The breeze and noise recede; the pavements dry. The flowers in the raised bed are caught in a vortex, then settle, motionless.

When you were young, you thought the world ceased to exist when you closed your eyes. You'd experiment with the length of your blinks, holding them longer and longer. When does a blink become *Close your eyes and go to sleep, Lexi?* You weren't sure.

You'd squeeze them tight and edge around the room using furniture to guide you. If you were touching something, it couldn't disappear, could it? Because you'd confirm the exact moment the world wasn't real anymore.

Sometimes you'd forget your eyes were shut and call frantically for your mother, who'd scoop you into the safety of her arms.

"Just open your eyes," she'd say softly, and you'd cry with relief.

Open your eyes.

Your eyes aren't shut. Finn's were, and when he opened them, *he* disappeared.

A whine emits from within you, like a wounded animal, evolving into a growl, then a yell. Every swallowed down emotion rises. You've been patient, optimistic, acquiescent. You've banged on doors, and you've sat quietly. You've searched for answers; you've tried to find a way out. What else is there?

"Why me? I don't understand any of this!"

You pick up a large rock from the road and hurl it at the car, reveling in the smashing sound it creates. You form a fist and pound on the bonnet. You rock the car, thrusting your body against it—it bounces a little on its tires but nothing more. You want so much to flip it over, to have the raw strength to expel every ounce of the frustration racing around you.

Tears slide down your face. You snatch them away with the back of your hand.

And when your energy is depleted, you slide down the driver's side door and sit among the debris.

"Have you finished?" Finn would say pompously, if he were here and not in some other reality.

Oh, Finn—how could you have forgotten about him? He looked so grey and defeated. Poor Finn. Is he waiting for you to come home? Has he been searching for you? His life put on hold, the way yours is, until you're reunited. How sad that is, the both of you all alone.

What would Finn do?

He'd say, "Bloody hell, I need a drink."

So, you stand and leave the wreckage of the car behind and walk to the pub half-way up the street. The door's locked, so you smash a window and haul yourself inside. The odor of stale beer and sweat assaults you. It takes a moment for your eyes to acclimatize to the dimness. At the bar, you open a bottle of wine and take a glass from the shelf.

The first sip is heaven—crisp and cold. You open the door and sit on the steps, and right now the heat doesn't feel so bad. It feels like a lovely afternoon on the longest day—a few drinks here, moving on to eat somewhere, a few more drinks. Even the deserted street doesn't seem quite so desolate as it has done. It's developed a serenity, an indulgence.

You pour another glass of wine and rest back against the door jamb, wondering what the day will bring.

CHAPTER TWENTY

FINN

When things happen that are out of your control—a loved one departing unexpectedly, for example—there's always a *what-if*, another path you might have taken had they stayed.

Sometimes, if he closes his eyes and opens them quickly, he catches glimpses of this alternate life—of Lexi lounging in the sun reading a book or sitting at the table drinking wine while he cooks, streaks of grey hair glinting, soft creases around her eyes. For a second, these moments are very real.

The house is too full to hide away on the longest day, this year. Full of teenagers and music and laughter. And Finn wants none of it. He buys his customary bottle of Jack Daniel's and stands indecisively at the foot of the stairs.

"Really? After all these years, you're still …?" Arms crossed, scowling, eyes glinting with resentment. Tiny lines form above her lips; a furrow appears between her eyebrows. "I don't understand why…" She throws her hands in the air. "Just, *why?* After all this time, all these years, and she's still"—tapping her temples— "in here."

"I can't…" He avoids her penetrating gaze. It's usually the kids on the receiving end of her chastisement.

"There's never an answer, is there? Do I mean nothing to you?"

"You know that's not—"

"No. I *don't*. Why would I know? You never tell me. You're as secretive and maddening as you've always been. You and *Lexi*." She spits out the name as if she can't bear it in her mouth a moment longer. "What about me? Where do I fit in?"

"Amber, please." Her pain tears into him, yet he doesn't know where to begin. Lost and uncertain, he's immobile, caught in a web of memories. He wants to sweep her into his arms and explain, but those words won't come.

"You know what?" She bites her lip, restraining the anger within her. "Go. Just go."

He glances around. "Go where?" He takes a step but senses it might be the wrong thing to do.

"Anywhere. I don't care. Get out of this house, and ..." She stops herself. She holds her hands, palms facing him. Resisting his lack of comprehension, reflecting his confusion back to him. "Just get this out of your system."

For once and for all hangs in the air, unsaid. This is the final warning. His composed and devoted wife has reached the end of her tether.

Finn packs an overnight bag while Amber watches with stony eyes and fends off the kids' questions, all the while wondering if this is what she meant, if he's failing some kind of test she's setting for him. He sits in the car outside the house waiting for her to chase after him, and when she doesn't, he drives. He drives across the bridge and up the dual carriageway, and when it turns into the M5, he carries on. He doesn't stop until he's hungry, and when he is, he checks into a cheap hotel on the edge of the motorway and sits alone for dinner.

The room is quiet, the tables dotted with a strange mix of people. Businessmen work on laptops with their meals beside them, a group of women heading out to the theatre share a bottle of Prosecco, an older couple eat silently, a father with two adult daughters discuss the museum they've just visited.

Finn leans back and sips his lager. His recollection of how he ended up here is disjointed and incomplete. Did he really just leave? Arguing with Amber is rare—she's usually so self-assured and steady, her temper slow to boil. Packing a bag and walking out, even more so. It was a mistake. He should call and let her know he's safe. Although she'll assume he is. She'll probably assume he's waiting at the end of the road and will return soon.

He messages: *In Taunton. Got a room for tonight. Home tomorrow.* His finger hovers over the send icon. *Love you xxx*

Taunton? How the hell did he end up here? She's going to be furious. He should leave, go home, face her wrath. But instead, he orders the first thing he sees on the menu and another lager.

The restaurant begins to fill. It's odd to be at a table without Amber leaning across with little comments about their fellow diners—noting a polite child or wondering if her meal will look as tempting as the one that man's eating. Or getting bored and arranging the cutlery so it's aligned and folding the napkins into airplanes or hats.

Finn hasn't spent a night away from her since Isla was born. That time, Georgie clambered into bed beside him because a thunderstorm was worrying him. He asked so many questions about his new baby sister and fell asleep in his father's arms mid-sentence.

Awaiting Finn upstairs, in this homogeneous hotel with car headlights flashing past on the motorway, is a king-sized bed, and he wonders what he'll do with all the space.

It's been twenty years since Lexi went, which means nineteen years of plunging into this pit of anguish. It's nothing more than a habit now, a day to be marked yet without the despair and paranoia of those early years.

This year, there's Phoebe to think about too. She died a couple of months ago; a friend of hers, working her way through Phoebe's contact list, phoned him. Finn listened silently to the brief details of Phoebe's cancer and thanked the person for calling; no, he couldn't make the funeral, but he would be thinking of her.

He wonders if she was lonely, if he should have done more for her. He wonders if she yearned for answers which would never come, or if she'd come to terms with her loss. Does anyone ever truly do that? Isn't there always a part of you expecting your loved one to walk through the door again?

In his room after dinner, Finn holds the bottle of Jack but doesn't open it. He tilts it side to side, watching the golden liquid clinging to the glass, and tucks it away in his bag.

No more.

***

Amber has scratched the kids' heights into the door jamb of their respective bedrooms since their first birthdays. Finn hates it. He feels shackled to the house for the sake of sentiment. How could they possibly move and leave behind such important milestones? Amber laughs when he grumbles while Isla stands patiently, keen to see how much she's grown.

"Twelve now, Dad," she says with glee, stretching herself as tall as possible, rising onto tiptoes while Amber pushes her back down. "Almost a teenager!"

The way she says this is mildly ominous and Finn wonders what she has in store for them.

In contrast, Georgie slouches petulantly when it's his turn the following February. Quiet, sensible; he observes, notes everything, choosing his moment to step into the fray. Pinky and the Brain, Finn muses with a smirk—Isla's whirlwind of activity alongside Georgie's sullen poise. If they collaborated, they'd be an unstoppable force.

"Stand straight, Georgie." Amber has to reach up to gouge the notch for the first time.

"George," he says.

"Sorry, *George*."

Finn stands behind her and gestures for him to cooperate. He does, and the mark is made.

"Do we have to do this *every* year?"

"Until you stop growing."

"Eighteen. No more after that."

Amber weighs the offer. Three more years. "Okay. I doubt you'll grow much more after that anyway."

"You should start doing Dad," he says with a wicked grin. "He's old now—you could see how much he shrinks."

"Oi!"

But Georgie's right. Finn's almost sixty. And sixty is old. He's mostly grey and the lines around his eyes are deep and permanent. In the morning it takes several minutes for his vision to focus on the jumping lines of his alarm clock; he groans when he sits down or gets into bed at night. The walk to work takes longer than it used to. His favorite Indian takeaway gives him indigestion.

And yet, it's no age at all. People run marathons at sixty. They travel, and take up new hobbies, or go back to studying. If he lives to ninety, he has another third of his life ahead of him. It's not old enough to make an issue of it, the way it once was.

One Tuesday in July, Amber says, "It's your birthday soon. What do you fancy doing? We could have a party."

"Oh, I don't think so." He lowers the book he's reading and peers over his glasses. "How about a quiet meal, just you and me, somewhere fancy?"

"But you're going to be sixty. It's a big thing."

Finn thinks: no, it isn't—it only means I haven't died yet. And he thinks: most people get to sixty, it's not an achievement.

"We could go away for the weekend, to that hotel in Dorset we could never afford. Your parents can have the kids."

"Let me make a fuss—you deserve it."

Finn thinks having a *fuss* made is for kids, for turning one or thirteen, or eighteen—for scratching the next stage of their lives into the woodwork and looking forward to the future. There's no stage after sixty, apart from deterioration and decline, and who wants to celebrate that?

"You know I'll do it anyway," Amber says, wrapping her arms around his shoulders and stretching to kiss his cheek. "I promise I won't make it too raucous or"—she smirks, with a wink—"you know, fun."

How did he get here? In this house with this wonderful woman, and kids who make him so proud every day? When he was alone in his old house, closed up to the world with the bleakness that overcame him, he was certain life would be colorless and stagnant forever. Indeed, before Lexi, when Claire left him for someone else, he'd been sure of the same. And he found Lexi. Just as he found Amber.

His beloved, amazing Amber who stopped the cycle beginning again, who he would give anything to, because *she* deserved it.

Including a party, the party which she's already deep in preparation for. There are flurries of emails and brown-boxed parcels, and surreptitious phone calls which halt when he enters a room.

On the day of his sixtieth birthday—old and decrepit—he lies in bed because Amber had arranged for them both to have the day off work. The kids deliver breakfast on a tray before going to school, and they spend a lazy morning together.

"Are you happy?" she asks, curling into him, skin against skin, warm and sweaty.

"I wish we could stay like this." His hand caresses her waist, his fingers probe the soft flesh of her stomach.

"Do you really mind about the party?"

"No, I'm glad you did it." And he rolls towards her, scooping her into his arms again.

***

There are about twenty people, when Finn counts them up, and he's surprised he knows so many. A few from the pub, his colleagues from work, Dean and his wife and a few others from the rugby team. Previous animosity is tamed; time heals, isn't that what they say?

Among them all, Amber shines. She's laughing with Dean and Nat, allowing Dean to top up her glass with a coy, *Oh just a little*. She's discussing her dying pot-plant with one of the older blokes from the pub, then deep in conversation with one of Isla's friends' mums.

Finn, sixty, feels ancient.

The lights go out and Georgie carries in the cake. Guests who have been talking in the kitchen follow, and the room is suddenly, claustrophobically full of people singing "Happy Birthday." He blows out the candles, feeling ridiculous.

"Make a wish," someone calls. But what wish does he have that hasn't already been granted? He closes his eyes and pretends.

"Speech," says the same voice.

He laughs to disguise his irritation, softening as he glances at Amber who's watching with pride and love.

"I'd like to thank you all for coming. And, of course, my beautiful wife"—pause for the 'aww' which flows around the room— "for organizing such a wonderful evening." Amber flushes and does a little curtsey. "I've known some of you since school, which is a very long time indeed. So, well, thank you for putting up with me. Enjoy the cake."

As everyone peels back into their own little groups, the photo on the mantelpiece catches Finn's eye, glinting in the fairy lights Isla put up—the two of them dancing, oblivious to the rest of the world.

"Dance with me," he says, taking her hand.

He doesn't hear the music, or Georgie and Isla giggling with embarrassment, or notice the friends who've turned to watch. He feels Amber's body sway into his and breathes in the floral fragrance of her perfume. Her arms are tight around his torso, her head pressed against his chest. He can't imagine his life any different. He doesn't deserve to be this happy.

CHAPTER TWENTY-ONE

LEXI

There's an equanimity, a peace cocooning you. You slink, you saunter; you slide like water through the streets and along the paths and up and down the hills, and in and out of houses as if they were your own—which, you suppose, they are now. But you haven't been back home; *that* house is restless and hostile.

Stolen clothes are dumped in other people's bathrooms or bedrooms as you tire of the ones you're wearing and need a change. You eat cake from their cupboards and biscuits from their novelty tins, despite not being hungry, *never* being hungry. You rummage their fridges for plated-up leftovers from last night's family meal. You snag on *last night* because *last night* is important—*was* important—although you can't remember why.

Last night you were with Finn, but as you try to pin down the details they flutter away.

The fog is cloaking everything, snatching at the edges of your life. As your thoughts and memories are cast off, they tether themselves to lampposts and garden gates, they rest on benches and against the rough stone walls which once formed the town's boundary. They're the stones left on pavements and postboxes and on car roofs; pieces of yourself discarded to lighten the burden. You've been saying goodbye without even realizing.

Many circuits of town ago, you walked past the leisure center and pressed your nose against the glass to view the swimming pool. You imagined immersing yourself in the cool water. You walked away, that first time, but returned, because you always return. This time, you smashed the glass of a side exit and peeled away the shards before climbing through. You broke the alarm, too, because the whirring-whining siren rang out along the playing field and through the streets with nothing to dampen it.

You come back often. Standing at the edge of the pristine surface in your borrow-pilfered swimming costume, you raise your hands above your head and dive in. Nothing spectacular, but each time becoming smoother and straighter—you've trained regularly, you found books on technique at the library.

You cut through the water, counting off the seconds it takes in your head. Behind you, waves run in rigid lines towards the edges and double back on themselves. It's exhilarating—the freedom, the lightness of your body being held in the water, the release of simply being.

Out of the water, your body is heavy and exhausted. You heave yourself onto the side of the pool and your bones ache from the effort. You try to sleep, lying in the shade of a tree in the park or in someone's freshly made bed, but it never comes.

You catch sight of yourself in the window separating the pool from the café—hunched over and ageing, your eyes bleak and desperate, your cheeks concaved. It's not the way you remember yourself. Is this what the fog is doing to you, sucking life from every cell of your body? You resemble your grandmother in the months before she died, a shadow of herself, a vague outline of the independent woman she used to be.

Gradually, as you stare at yourself, people emerge behind the glass. You look through your reflection to the shapes sharpening from hazy figures to normal people doing normal things, just as they've done before—reappearing as if they haven't been missing all this time. They're sitting and talking, or queuing, or gathering their kids and checking their bags. Toddlers are running around with wet hair and toweling robes.

So many people, so much movement and commotion again. The bustle is harsh, too much to bear after the repose you've come to accept. You step back from the glass, the swimming pool still empty. You step back into the shadows and around the corner, quiet as a mouse.

One by one, they vanish. The building resumes its solitude and serenity. The anxiety you were just this moment holding on to releases, and you sigh. Death, or this fraction of a second after your last breath—if that's what this is—this final moment of awareness which is an eternity, suits you. Death. Is that what this is?

***

Lying on the small pebbled beach at the Waterside, beneath the bridges out of town, the sun stings your legs which are neither burnt nor tanned. You listen to the silence as if it were an opera. It's not actually silent. Each part of the town has its own vibration in the air, an almost imperceptible hum.

Finn—or at least a ghostly manifestation of Finn—sits beside you and holds your hand. He's stopped talking to you; you've forgotten the sound of his voice. Sometimes his absence shatters you; at others, he's so distant, he's just a name, as if you'd plucked him from the telephone directory. There's nothing in between, no easy grief-quieted moments where he painlessly occupies your thoughts. Each memory of him is fought for—you will *not* forget, *cannot* forget. The love grows more intrinsic with every passing—

No, not *passing*; nothing is passing. It is, and will ever be, 6:05 with its long shadows stretching across the barren streets.

The fog forms an increasingly tighter circle around you yet retains its strict distance. You can measure it in feet now, a diameter of thirty at most; when you walk, the circle moves with you. You've forgotten what the view was like. You've forgotten the curve of the horizon and the colors of flowers in full bloom. Behind you, the terrace of houses is hidden, and the statue of Brunel in his smart stovepipe hat is being consumed.

The river no longer exists, save for the very edge. You inch forward until your bare toes dip into the warm water. The tide would normally lap against you with a soft crash and *slush* as it ebbed and flowed over the sand, but now it simply distorts the shape of your feet like glass. You take a pebble, smooth and flat, and throw. It skims the surface, although the water is unrippled.

"Did you see that, Finn? Three bounces!"

You take a sip of the lager you poured at the pub across the road—still slightly too frothy because you didn't angle the glass far enough, you obviously need a bit more practice. At some previous point, you broke the glass panel and unbolted the locked door from inside, allowing access whenever you're down this way. What else would you do? Sit *without* a beer on this beautiful day?

Beside you are the grapes you discovered in a kitchen, and brie from its neighboring house. Later, you might search for dessert, perhaps an ice-cream or a fruit trifle. Someone will have something yummy they're not going to eat.

The crackling, snapping sound from inside the fog is faint yet constant, a reminder.

You pull the brie from its triangle and squish it into your mouth with a grape, creamy and sharp at the same time. The juice oozes down your chin and you wipe it with the back of your hand, leaving a sticky streak across your cheek.

With your legs stretched out, you lean against the steps dividing the path from the tiny beach. You could walk or search for a cool room to doze in or find a long engaging book to read, or music to listen to. But it all feels like too much effort now.

The fog steps nearer.

The heat weighs you down, pushing you further and further into the sand; your legs are weary from the thousands of miles you must have walked by now. You sip the lager.

And nearer.

You stare into it, dazzled by the hypnotic vapor swirling around, watching the shapes in the shadows it creates within itself.

Images form. Your first day of school accompanied by your proud parents; your first kiss; a camping holiday in France. Friends from school, from work, Mila, and Vanessa, and Aunt Phoebe, and ...

So many people you haven't thought about for so long. So long, and just a second ago.

And nearer.

Static raises the hairs on your arms.

It tingles, like a finger running delicately along your spine.

"It's time, isn't it?" you say.

But you don't want to leave. You're content—happy, even.

Growing taller and thicker, the fog stretches above you, blocking the heat of the sun. The chill starts at your feet and rises higher, higher. Your calves, your thighs, your stomach. Icy, shivering. Your arms and throat and head.

Standing, you wipe the rough sand from the trousers you're wearing, all the while eyeing the fog, daring it to make the first move. You take small, calculated steps backwards. Holding your breath. Waiting.

Time, unmoving. The hands of your watches, the sun, frozen in place. You, alone, in this impossible town. And the fog, its permanence and reassurance, its protection and relief. The silence consistent and uniform.

"I don't want to go."

So, you run.

You run.

You run.

The piles of stones around town have accumulated—your pain and anger divested, one tiny memory at a time. Not a single road is unadorned by these testaments. It's easy to run when you're not beleaguered by the past, when you're as light and fluid as the fog itself.

From the narrow alleys behind houses and between estates, and the brown grass of the playing fields, to the seclusion of the small dell with the stream trickling through it and the railway line following the curve of the hills, the fog leaves nowhere to hide. It curls around the trees and hangs in wisps from branches and pours along the streets as if flowing from a cauldron.

You run.

All around you. Slinking closer, ominous and inevitable. How could you possibly stay here? Life doesn't work that way. You can't avoid your fate, or step aside from it, however briefly.

Yet, you're still running. Legs pounding, heart beating. Flying through the streets.

When you stop, you are home.

CHAPTER TWENTY-TWO

FINN

On an ordinary Tuesday, several years ago, Sophie Sutton woke from a nightmare which wasn't really a nightmare but a long-suppressed childhood memory of watching a man digging in his garden in the middle of the night.

She doesn't recall why she was up at that time—perhaps her parents disturbed her when they came home from an evening out to relieve the babysitter, or she needed the bathroom and became distracted. Or perhaps the gentle rasp of a shovel being driven into the soil roused her. Either way, the moon shone so brightly she thought it must be morning time. She stood on the small toy box in front of her window and peered through the gap in her curtains. The moon was indeed as luminous as the sun. Except she could also see stars springing out from the black sky.

Down in the garden next door, someone was moving around. A tall hedge blocked some of the view—the figure moved in and out of the shadows. The girl clutched her pink doggy, but she couldn't stop watching. Every so often, the man would lean on the shovel, wipe his forehead, and glance along the row of unlit windows looming over him.

The child would duck, holding her breath so the tiny sound on the sluggish, humid air wouldn't draw his attention.

The memory, at this point, wilts and the woman wonders if perhaps her mother came in to tuck her back into bed, if she'd snuggled into her duvet and earned herself a second bedtime story. Perhaps she'd told her mother about the man in the garden, and her mother hugged her and told her not to be silly.

On an ordinary day, a few days ago, the same woman walked into a solicitor's office above the pizza place on Fore Street to discuss her father's will, and stood face-to-face with her old neighbor, a scary man called Finn.

There was no mistaking it, although he was a deflated, grey-haired version of the man who left his house every Saturday afternoon in rugby kit and who filled his car when he sat inside so it appeared there'd be no room for anyone else. Slouching, floundering in a suit which seemed slightly too big for him, this was the giant who yelled when she accidentally kicked her ball into his garden and knocked on their door when she made too much noise. This was the man from her dream.

Every muscle in her body tightened; she was four years old again, wide-eyed, desperate to hide behind her mother's legs.

"Hello. Can I help you?" he asked, turning away from an open filing cabinet when he heard her enter.

She wanted to run but had no idea why. Her throat was dry. The unexpected warmth of the room contrasting with the icy October wind outside made her dizzy. She unzipped her coat to cool herself down, but then she was exposed and self-conscious. She pulled the coat around her and found a hard surface to rest against.

"Appointment," she whispered, but the details escaped her, even the name of the person she was due to meet. It wasn't *him*, was it?

"Name?"

She gawped blankly. She didn't know.

"What's your name?"

She coughed before attempting to speak again. "Sophie Sutton."

She watched carefully in case he showed signs of recognition and asked after her family. Had they been friends? Did he lend her father his lawn mower while her mother and the nice lady he lived with swapped recipes over the back fence? Did they have a glass of sherry together at Christmas while their respective lunches were cooking?

Finn bent down to the computer and smiled again. "Take a seat, Miss Sutton. Can I offer you a drink while you wait? Tea, coffee?"

She shook her head. "No. Thank you." Her skin bristled under his gaze as she took a seat on the chair he indicated.

"Are you okay, Miss Sutton? You look a little unwell. Can I get you some water?"

She shook her head again, and Finn returned to the filing cabinet; but she couldn't shake the edgy feeling. It wasn't anything she could pinpoint, just a nagging desire to run. She stared at the geometric-pattered carpet, the shapes floating in front of her, her eyes blurring. She stood abruptly, catching her bag on the chair and making a thudding sound.

"I'm sorry. I have to go. I've remembered I ... I'll make another appointment. Now's not a good time." And she fled down the narrow staircase, ignoring his concerned entreaties to stay, and out onto the street. Fresh air filled her lungs and the giddiness abated.

But the nightmares returned.

***

In a town of less than 20,000 inhabitants, you come across the same people over and over. You might not know everyone by name, but you'll pass them at the bus stop as you walk to work, you'll talk to them as they serve you in the butchers or chemist. There's a fair chance you'll happen across faces you recognize in the doctor's waiting room or at the gym, and you might say a few words to pass the time. Or you'll know someone who knows a lot of people, and they'll gossip about them, and the names might stick in your head.

Some people, despite the intervening years, might recall there was once a young woman called Lexi Peters who vanished overnight, although no one ever knew what became of her. Her boss was left in the lurch, her friends had no inkling where she'd gone, her aunt received no calls to say she was safe. For one summer, everyone knew Lexi's name, everyone talked about her. Reckless theories ran with abandon, the way these things sometimes do, but they waned. Something else took her place.

Finn could have done anything after Lexi went. He could have travelled, as he told her he always wanted to. He could have moved away—to London or New York—and leached into an anonymous life.

He could have remained a recluse.

But he didn't do any of those things. He unexpectedly fell in love. He got married and had two children who he can't imagine life without. He cheers from the sidelines when his son scores a try and listens to his daughter practice her guitar. He holds his wife's hand when they walk together and, on the face of it, he's a perfectly ordinary man.

***

After a few more nights of terrifying dreams and lying awake in the early hours watching headlights create shadows on her ceiling and listening to radiator pipes creaking—and, yes, debating the irrationality of it—Sophie Sutton phones the police and tells them about the vegetable patch in the garden next to her childhood home.

The following day, she's at the police station repeating her story.

"So, you saw your neighbor, Finn Carmichael, digging in the garden late at night?" PC Maddox reads back through her notes and Sophie nods. "Did you see his face? Did you know him as your neighbor at that point?"

"I think so. I'd forgotten all about it until I saw him at the solicitor's the other day." Or was it a mistake, a silly nightmare she's recalling as real? Kids make up things—her parents fondly remember her heightened imagination. She cups her face with both hands. What if she's wrong? She shouldn't have said anything. "It was a long time ago. I'm sorry, I think I'm wasting your time."

"It's not a problem. At this point, I'm just taking a few details. We'll cross-check it with the information we have on the case and establish if we need to investigate further. If it's an innocent misunderstanding, the matter will be dropped, no harm done."

PC Maddox produces a satellite image of the houses and their gardens and places it on the desk between them. "Which was your house, and where was the man digging?"

Sophie points to the long oblong on the left of her old house and indicates an area right on the boundary line. "Here. I was looking from my bedroom window. This tree was smaller, so I saw more of him than I would now, I guess." She shrugs.

"You're doing great."

"I don't remember much about when she went missing, but my parents talked about her every so often. I guess she'd have only been a couple of years older than I am now."

PC Maddox nods solemnly. She's around the same age, too.

Three days later, two police officers are digging the area where the vegetable patch used to be. It's been re-lawned, with a dilapidated goalpost growing into it. They cut the grass into squares, piling them to one side so they can be replaced later. They use implements to scratch at the earth, a delicate and meticulous process, every inch scoured, nothing discounted.

Neighbors peer from their back bedroom windows or find reason to be in their gardens and glance over their fences. They swap low-voiced commentary with the people who live further down the terrace. Within an hour, news of something ominous happening has spread half-way across town.

Eventually, one of the officers unearths a bone and calls the other to examine it. Heads bent in somber discussion, they slide the item into a bag.

A tent is erected in the garden. The young homeowners—a couple with a three-year-old child—are briefed to stay with friends. It all seems to happen so fast, and Sophie forgets she was the catalyst. What if she's wrong? People will know it's her—they'll stare at her, point her out to others, laugh at her stupidity. *That guy?* He's just a middle-aged man, why would you pick on him?

Sophie goes to work but spends the day distracted. She sits in the staff room at lunchtime and bites her nails. She imagines the night she slipped from her bed, woken by the strange thudding sounds, and looked out of the window because the moon was too bright. She sees the dark outline of the man digging the hole as distinctly now as she did then. In her mind, he turns and smiles at her.

Lexi had been digging, too, a few days before that. She was planting carrots and showed Sophie the tiny seeds. She said if it was okay with Sophie's mum, she could come and help at the weekend.

Perhaps Finn was simply doing the same thing, planting carrots.

PC Maddox said she'd call if there was any news. At 2:15 p.m. on the third day, there hasn't been any.

CHAPTER TWENTY-THREE

LEXI

You're home, but you're not. Standing in the hall, the stairs are ahead of you, the front door behind, because you've just walked through it. But it's not your house. The lemon-colored walls are papered with large red flowers instead; the newly laid floor is dull and tarnished.

You opened your front door, because it's where you ended up when you stopped running, but this is not your house.

It's cold, dark. After all this time in the sweltering sunshine. Behind you, the street—your street, definitely *your* street—is spotted with the orange glow of streetlights and houselights. How long has it been since you saw a light, needed a light?

You're back. You've actually come back!

The fog caught up with you, you presume, but rather than the violent repatriation you were expecting, you're just here. As though none of it even mattered.

Back with people and the sound of cars and children roaming in small gangs, bouncing balls and screeching nonsense at each other. Back with the wind gusting through the trees in the neighbors' gardens—branches bare, as though this is winter rather than the summer it's been forever. Every sound is an explosion; every movement feels like it's being displayed on an IMAX.

There's a draught coming from the kitchen, and you go to investigate, passing furniture which isn't yours and piles of toys shoved into a corner. You pass several people on the way. People you avoid by pressing yourself against the wall as they rush back and forth. Why so many people in this house which may or may not be yours?

In the kitchen, a policeman is leaning against the open back door, hands behind his back, looking at his feet.

"Um, excuse me. What's going on? I live here. Has something happened?" Your unease rises. So much commotion after such tranquility. It's hard to comprehend. You want your empty streets and houses back; you want the peace and lethargy.

He says nothing, embarrassed perhaps, unaware you'd arrived and unsure how to explain. Someone else, with more authority, will be tasked with talking to you, once they track you down. Currently, no one seems interested in you, and for that you're grateful. One adjustment at a time is all you can deal with.

You continue into the garden. The air is early morning crisp and frost coats the grass; drizzle hangs on cobwebs, creating an intricate pattern within the wooden trellis. Your skin is cold, but you aren't. At the end of the garden, a large white tent has been erected. Two people in hooded overalls and face masks are kneeling beside it.

Just outside the door are two women, neither wearing police uniform—one mumbling into her phone, the other staring into the garden with an air of gravity.

"Am I allowed out here?"

You don't wait for an answer. Your steps are slow, as if you have to fight for each one, as if trying to stop yourself from running in the other direction. Anxiety wraps around you like a slowly tightening bandage.

"What's going on?" you ask one of the overalled people, but he doesn't reply. He adjusts the camera strap around his neck and studies the screen, turning away from you. They're all so focused—none of them laughs, none of them shares the usual small talk you'd have with a colleague.

Inside the tent, a third person is retrieving items from a hole and placing them on a blue plastic sheet. Sallow, mud-covered bones. They're placed in such a way to mimic a leg and an arm. With two hands, she carefully places a skull on the sheet. She's talking as she does this, but you can't make out what she's saying.

The photographer smiles grimly and nods. He takes several photos while crouched, then stands for more. Other items appear from the hole inside the tent—broken bits of pot, a deflated ball, scraps of material, small bones which are set out as fingers on the end of the arm.

"Excuse me," you say a little louder than before, turning to the second man. "Please help. I think I'm lost. Where's Finn? Have you seen Finn?"

Luci, with his shrewd emerald eyes and single white paw, watches from the end of the garden. When you spot him, he pads towards you and brushes against your leg. You bend to stroke him, and he purrs. "Hey, Pussy Cat, do you have any idea what's going on?"

Snap goes the camera.

"Well," says the second man with a protracted sigh. "I think that's definitive, don't you?"

A long bone is laid on the sheet. A bone with slivers of leather at one end. *Snap.* Slivers of leather with two watch faces tangled up in it.

You grasp the two watches on your wrist, both right where they should be. And yet, undeniably there, on the ground, excavated from the depths of the hole.

You're not lost after all.

And you're not standing on the frosted grass in the drizzle. You're on the plastic sheet; decomposing fragments form the shape of the body you used to be.

Snap.

You can't avert your eyes; compelled to watch, drawn to the horror uncovered. There's no one to notice you and pull you away as they would if this were a film. No one to comfort you or shield your eyes. The woman in the hole climbs out and they cover the pieces of you with the plastic sheet you're lying on, as if swaddling a child, and place you in a black body bag. You soak in every detail: the diligence and respect with which they treat your body, the short pause with their heads bowed.

They carry you through the back gate, along the narrow alleyway, and around the corner to the waiting black ambulance. A tear rolls down your cheek, then another.

Neighbors are gathered, although nobody you recognize. Some talk in low voices; others cover their mouths, eyes wide with astonishment. Several hug briefly, offering solace to each other; one wipes a tear from her eye.

The van doors slam shut, and you jump. You reach out with an arm which isn't actually there, which no one else can see. The green varnish on your nails, freshly painted years ago to brighten your dreary work suit, glimmers while everything else is grey.

Yesterday. Painted *yesterday.*

Fog descends. It all makes sense now. And it's coming to an end.

"Finn," you say out loud. Such an alien word on your tongue, as all words are now. Once, the best word.

CHAPTER TWENTY-FOUR

FINN

Finn switches on the radio. He fills the kettle and sets out two mugs while Amber nudges the kids awake. He listens to their indignant complaints and her no-nonsense replies. She's on her phone when she enters the kitchen, scrolling through her social feeds or one of the news apps, he supposes. The older he gets the less he understands all these things that pop up. Amber, on the other hand, relishes new technology and loves learning from the kids.

"The police are digging up one of the gardens in your old road," she says casually.

"What?"

Color drains from his face. A chill spreads across him, numbing his fingers and toes.

"Yeah, someone who lives there posted this photo." She holds the phone out to him.

A knot punches into his stomach. The kitchen swirls around him. He forces himself to take long, slow breaths. Counts them. Focuses on the clock, on the mellifluous rhythm of the second hand. The gap between ticks seems to elongate.

He sees her face, conjured up from that long-ago night. Another lifetime. He's filled with the rage and panic which seized him back then. His hands curl themselves into a fist. And he watches the clock, the lengthening gap between ticks.

"Cool!" Georgie runs down the stairs and bursts into the room. "Matt says they're digging up dead bodies in his neighbor's garden." He emits a ghostly wail and wafts his hands over his mother until she bats him away.

"Yeah, right. Not in *this* town." Isla follows him, yawning. She stands at the fridges and lets cold air rush out while she decides what she wants. "Nothing happens here. There won't be any dead bodies."

"Nah, look. Matt says they've found a skeleton." He thrusts his phone towards his sister, pushing it into her face until she jabs him in the ribs, and he backs off—behavior which usually draws rebuke from Amber.

Finn watches silently from his seat at the table. The rushing and fighting and mayhem. He imagines this life crumbling around him like a jigsaw puzzle being broken up.

The kids, pushing each other out of the way as they dance around the room with cereal and bowls.

Amber, stock-still in the middle of the room, staring at her phone. Staring at the photo.

She frowns, moving thoughts around her head.

Finn waits. Pulse racing, adrenaline pumping. Watching the seconds.

Amber closes her eyes to concentrate, moving instinctively out of the way as Isla passes behind her. Conversations replaying, recollections emerging, linking together, making sense. From uncertainty to realization; frown to shock to open-mouthed horror.

The phone falls from her fingers. "Oh my god. Lexi." It's not a question.

"Who's Lexi?" Isla asks through a mouthful of cereal, and Finn grimaces at the name on her lips.

"Both of you, go and get dressed, please," Amber says quietly.

"I just came down."

"You have to sign this letter."

"Go upstairs," she says through gritted teeth, eyes on Finn.

"I'm eating!"

"I'm hungry!"

Amber claps her hands once, so loud it echoes. "Go to your rooms!"

The silence in the kitchen is hostile as Amber watches the kids push and shove each other up the stairs. She waits until their doors are slammed shut, then closes the kitchen door and turns to Finn, summoning whatever strength she needs.

"They're digging at your old house."

Finn shakes his head in confusion, in denial. His old life and his new smashing together.

"Talk to me."

He looks up, but not at Amber. He's miles away from Amber.

"They're looking for Lexi."

Her voice is distant, drifting. He struggles to hear her.

It's coming—the end of everything. He's been waiting for such a long time, and he's tired. He thought it would happen sooner, and when it didn't, he relaxed, allowed himself to feel safe, comfortable. Indeed, life before Amber is an illusion—a dream he once had, a novel he read. It's not his life; it's not him.

He should have remained alone after Lexi. He should have stayed in that house to look after her.

Amber, standing in front of him, waiting for answers, is frozen—mid-sentence, mid-frown. And what can he say? How can he possibly begin to explain?

He takes his coat from the peg and leaves the house. There's a nasty wind today, blowing from the north. The sun hangs on the trees, leaving a trail of purple and orange as it rises. To the west, the sky is still inky—dawn doesn't appear to be in any hurry this morning. Finn zips up his jacket and takes gloves from the pockets. He should have grabbed his hat; his ears are already stinging.

Amber calls after him, running down the garden steps in her dressing gown and slippers. She stands in the middle of the road and yells his name. A neighbor looks across in surprise and follows Amber's gaze to Finn who's striding away.

"Everything okay?" the neighbor asks, and Amber stares without comprehending the question.

He's going *there*, of course. To the house, to see for himself. Because it can't be real, can it? Perhaps *this* life is the illusion, jigsaw-pieced together from Hallmark movies and other people's happiness. The perfect family, the ideal wife, kids he couldn't bear to live without.

It's been so very long since he was last there even the route feels alien. Shadows follow him along the road, closing in on him. Ghosts of things he'd rather not remember. The eyes of people he passes are dark and accusing—have they ever stopped being so? Has he merely overlooked it as family life wrapped around him like a protective sheath? His footsteps echo, slow and erratic, as he forces himself onward.

He turns the corner into his old road and wavers. The trees are taller, more than there used to be. Some of the houses have been extended. A corner of someone's garden has an ugly new-build forced into the tiny space. People have embraced the requirement for more plants and flowers, to encourage nature to thrive, to bring the bees back. The tarmac on the road is pot-holed and bumpy; weeds spurt from gaps in the curb.

Two police cars are parked outside the house when he reaches it, and a throng of people have amassed. A Scene of Crime Officer wearing white overalls is removing items from a van; a uniformed PC is guarding the front door, stamping her feet and rubbing warmth into her hands. They exchange a few words, even a joke, and the PC holds the tape which criss-crosses the garden up high for him to slink under. Finn stands on the opposite side of the road, camouflaged among the other onlookers.

The house looks normal from here, almost as he remembers. But it's not the front being violated, is it? In the photo Georgie's friend took, police are plundering the back garden, with a white tent erected on one side. The grass has become a swampy mess after all their digging and recent rain.

Lexi stands beside him. Except she doesn't, of course. Her fragrance drifts across his path but he realizes he's imagining it. She used to wear that scent all the time, one which reminded him of the sea.

There'd been a blistering heatwave during those last few days with her. She lay naked in bed, the curves of her body silhouetted in the moonlight while he watched sleeplessly. During the day, she floated around the house in tiny vest and shorts because she couldn't bear the weight of fabric against her skin. Her perfume filled the air, then as it does now. How easily it's all coming back; how softly the years fall away. He sighs as the memories infiltrate.

In the corner of his eye, he catches her—matching his stance and demeanor, gazing at their house with unease and melancholy.

"Lexi?" he whispers, anticipating a reply. He tuts to himself. "Silly old man."

The road is soundless, the wind tapers, as the black ambulance pulls out of the side road and slowly disappears out of sight. A few people bow their heads; one makes the sign of the cross and clasps their hands together in prayer, it seems.

And then they disperse, ready to start their day. Finn remains until he's the only one left, then he too walks away.

CHAPTER TWENTY-FIVE

LEXI

It was your idea to go out for dinner after work instead of going home, although you don't remember why. The day had started badly and continued in that fashion. You wanted to quit your job and tell your colleagues exactly what you thought of them. You felt trapped by it all and needed to escape. You wanted a distraction, perhaps that was reason enough.

The restaurant was quiet when you arrived. You were early because you finished work at least an hour before Finn, so you expected to be. Maybe you wandered around the shops for a while; maybe you popped into a pub on the way. Either way, you were still early. A couple on the other side of the room drew your attention—holding hands, ignoring the menu, deep in conversation—and you recalled a time when you and Finn were just like that. You sipped a small glass of Sauvignon Blanc and pretended not to be watching.

When Finn arrived, you were slightly irritated, almost forgetting you'd invited him. You didn't want to share this moment of serenity with anyone.

"This was a nice idea," he said, bending to kiss you. "Had a good day?"

"I guess. You?"

"Yeah. Busy as always." He draped his jacket over the back of his chair and sat, scraping its legs across the tiled floor. The noise drilled into your skull.

A waitress appeared. Finn ordered a Coke while you asked for another glass of wine. "Actually, could I have a bottle?"

The bottle was for you alone; Finn didn't drink white.

"Well, if we're drinking, I'll have a beer instead. Thanks." When the waitress left, he said, "Unusual for you to be drinking on a school night."

"I just fancied it. You didn't have to join me." Defensive and riled. Did it really matter what you were drinking?

"No, it's all good." He perused the menu even though he always had the same Carbonara with chicken. He set it aside. "What's wrong?"

"Nothing."

"So, what's all this about?"

"Does there have to be a reason? Does everything have to have a sodding *reason?*"

"Lexi?"

The waitress returned and you leant back so she had room to place the beer and the bottle of wine on the table. You poured a large glass, almost to the brim, and gulped the wine.

"Steady."

You watched the pale liquid in the glass for a moment. "Did you know today's the anniversary of the day we met?"

"No." Finn raised his glass. "Happy anniversary."

"And here we are. Still."

"Well, that's a good thing, surely. We're celebrating. How long is it, five years?"

"Yeah. Five," Another glug, coughing as the alcohol hit the back of your throat.

"You could sound a little happier about it."

You glared at him, unable to conceal your disdain. "You know what—let's get drunk! Cheers." Another chug.

Finn didn't drink. "I'm driving, Lexi."

You giggled. "Oh yeah."

"For fuck's sake, Lexi. Tell me what's going on. Say whatever it is you want to say, I'm sick of these games."

A pause floated over the table. The clink of cutlery and glasses around the room was suppressed; the murmur of conversation ceased.

Your smile faded. "I wanted to travel. I was going to hand my notice in. I stayed because of you."

"I know. And I'm the luckiest man because—"

"You said you wanted to, as well. You said we'd go together and have all the amazing adventures I'd planned."

He nodded. "I did—"

"You lied."

"My job, Lexi ... You know how hard it was."

"Yes. Your job."

The meals arrived. Finn began to separate the chicken from the pasta, the way he always did, making piles and curling the spaghetti onto his fork. You didn't even look at your plate.

"It's not what I wanted," you said.

Finn frowned and raised his hand to call the waitress back.

"Not *this*." You circled your hand over the plate then broadened the gesture to encompass the table. "This. Us. I think," you whispered, wide-eyed with the shock of hearing such awful words escaping your lips. Words you'd kept inside for so long, pushing them away when they reared.

"You want to break up?"

"Yes. No!" You couldn't look at him, your eyes fixed instead on the glass in your hand. "I love you. But we're drifting. We don't do anything. You're grumpy and tired all the time."

Grumpy! You stifled a giggle. That made him sound like a granddad—grumpy Grandpa.

Another sip. "We didn't even book a holiday this year."

"My job—"

"It's not a fucking excuse. Everyone has jobs." You snorted. "That's *how* they can afford bloody holidays. We're coasting—we're living the same lives we were five years ago. My friends are having kids; we've never even discussed getting married."

"So, you want that now? You want kids?" He ran his fingers through his hair, suddenly thawing and allowing a smile. "Because I'd marry you in an instant. *You* resisted. You made me feel you were biding your time with me before someone better came along."

"When did I do that?"

He remained quiet, but his eyes bore into you.

"Finn, I love you."

The speed of your thoughts was baffling. Too many things all at once were cascading and you couldn't make sense of them. You loved him; you hated him. You wanted to be with him forever and couldn't wait to run away.

Finn pulled his hand away as you reached across the table. Your two watch faces glinted in the overhead light.

"The problem is you don't know what you want. *We're* not coasting—*you* are. Expecting everyone to coming running whenever you want them. Like the spoilt little princess you've always been."

"What the fuck did you call me?"

"You heard."

"Fuck you!" You jerked your arm with annoyance. Your sleeve caught on the fork, and it clattered to the floor.

People stared. The couple across the room held hands and smiled smugly. How you despised other people right then—strangers, friends, Finn. Especially Finn. Why couldn't they all just disappear and leave you alone?

"So, what the hell are we doing? What's the point, if this is how you feel?"

"Me? You brought it up. This is all on you." He grabbed your hands as you reached for the bottle again, preventing you from pouring another glass.

"You should eat something; you haven't touched your food."

"Get off me."

"You're drunk."

"So what? So what, *Finn?*"

At some point, you left the restaurant, Finn steering you through the maze of tables and out onto the street. Your steps faltered as you staggered and skipped after him. Drunk and reprimanded, he barely acknowledged you. The pavement blurred beneath your feet; the world spun way too fast.

He tried to hold your hand to guide you across roads, but you snatched it away which made you stumble. You giggled as cars beeped their horns and swerved around you.

"Come on, Lexi. Move."

Two Finns pushed you out of the way of a taxi. Two Finns seethed in front of you—lips pressed together, eyes fixed into a glower. Sometimes there were three of him, switching places and smashing back into one person when you concentrated.

"Where are we going? I'm hungry." Your head turned towards the burger van, your body followed, lured by the smell of grease and chips. Your stomach gurgled uncomfortably.

You'd wanted passion and ferocity from him. You'd wanted extravagant declarations of love.

If not that, an apology for tricking you so easily into this sedate, monotonous life with the wrong man.

Oh, no, that wasn't right. He wasn't the wrong man. How could you believe such a thing? Your inebriation tangled your thoughts and desires—you wanted him to hold you, to make it better.

What, then?

Do you remember?

It's all a blur, isn't it? An alcohol-induced fog. You had all these issues you wanted to discuss, but they became muddled up with hurtful and horrid things you'd never say when you were sober. The wine was supposed to give you courage, but you couldn't remember why you needed it in the first place.

Then you were home, in an instant—Finn opening the car door and hauling you out. Then you were in the kitchen, filling a glass from the tap and gripping the edge of the sink waiting for the retching sensation to pass. Behind you, Finn was talking, or yelling. Your jumbled head couldn't make sense of his words.

"Shut up!" You spun around and slapped him. So hard your palm stung, and the bright white shape of your fingers was stark on his cheek. Shock on both your faces. Oh yes, you remember that.

"Bitch." He grabbed your arm and pulled you towards him. His eyes locked with yours, fury against fury. He conceded first and turned to leave the room.

"We're talking." You yanked him back. Too big and heavy for you, he didn't budge, so you punched him—a mighty swing which caught his elbow.

"We're really not."

"Don't walk away from me!"

"We'll talk in the morning, when you've sobered up."

He was managing you, placating you. You didn't want to be mollified and soothed like a child. You wanted to fight and argue and be left breathless and exhausted. How dare he walk away. The throbbing in your head amplified, the queasiness exacerbated. You ran along the hall after him, glaring as he climbed the stairs.

"You never asked me to marry you. You stopped me traveling. You stuck me here in this stupid house."

"You feel stuck?" Half-way up, he towered over you, teetering. "You want to leave? Go ahead. There's the door."

It wasn't him teetering, it was you; swaying, clinging to the banister. Looking up made you dizzy. You stumbled up the stairs and grabbed his arm.

"Finn, please. I didn't mean ... I love you. You know I love you."

"Then why are you saying this? Why now? What's going on?"

You didn't know anymore. It had been so clear earlier, when your thoughts were making sense. You'd spoken to Vanessa on the phone. She'd settled into the notion of having a baby, after her panic a few weeks ago—her new-found poise and happiness flowed down the line. And you were jealous. Your aggravations with Finn intensified; the friction and rage gnawed at you.

He prised your fingers away, one at a time. Shouting at you to leave him alone.

"Finn, please ..."

"Lexi. Stop this. Lexi, leave me alone. Lexi—"

One moment, you were holding on to him. The next you were tumbling backwards.

CHAPTER TWENTY-SIX

FINN

After watching the black ambulance pull away from his old house, Finn goes home. He can't face the office today; surely no one would expect him to when his life is collapsing around him. The house is empty—the kids are at school, Amber will be at work, probably sitting and chatting to one of the regulars the way she used to chat to him.

He stands in the kitchen with the kettle in his hand. He puts it back down without filling it. Stares at it. All the breakfast things have been cleared away. It resembles a show home. Impossibly sterile and stark; the lingering emotions of this morning have been sanitized. His weariness is returning, the heaviness he felt when Lexi went. No, not went, died. Was killed. Murdered. No, not murdered—too harsh and final. That can't be what happened.

In the living room, he sits in his chair and waits. It's too late to run; he's too old. Would he have, though, if this had all happened years ago? Who knows? It doesn't matter anymore.

He thinks of Georgie and Isla—two people who wouldn't even exist if it weren't for him. What joy he brought into his world. He thinks of Amber, of the pain this will bring into hers. Of the security he's ripping away from the people he loves the most.

They won't understand. They shouldn't have to. He barely understands it himself. It isn't fair. He was happy.

Once, he loved Lexi more than anything in the world. How life changes. How it veers off on tangents and backtracks and plays itself over and over and always returns to the truth.

The photo on the mantelpiece—of him and Amber swaying on the tiny dancefloor at their tiny wedding—is facedown. She must have done that after he left this morning, refusing to witness the lies which have always been there. He picks it up and wipes dust from the glass with his sleeve. The silver frame is tarnished a little, like him, like the life he built up around him.

Amber's so young in this picture, eleven years his junior. Already he had suggestions of ageing—laughter lines around his eyes and thinning hair, a slight paunch which belied his insistence he was ready to play rugby again anytime he chose. What did she ever see in him? He should have walked away; it was a selfish indulgence to think he could live a normal life. Amber's not even fifty yet—young enough to start again.

"Finn." Amber stands at the living room door with her hands folded across her chest. Her face is red and tear marked.

"I thought you'd be at work."

"I was looking for you. I thought, maybe, you wouldn't be coming back."

He stares ahead, unable to meet her eye. The house shrinks with her in it.

"We have to decide what to tell the kids."

Oh, the children, his beautiful babies. He bites his lip and wipes a tear.

"Do you want me to phone your dad, your sister?"

"No."

Amber sits on the sofa and glances around the room. Her gaze lands on the photo on the mantelpiece and she turns towards the window instead. The river is a beautiful aquamarine today, still enough for two kayakers to spear themselves upstream.

"Did you do it?" Her voice is passive and steady—no emotion, none left. Facts. Just facts.

He says nothing.

"Oh." She clutches her mouth as if she's about to vomit and turns back to him. She stands and paces. With each turn she opens her mouth to speak, closing it again because there are no words. She glances at the photo on the mantelpiece. "Were we ever happy?"

"Oh yes. I loved you. I still do. I always will."

"How can I trust anything you say? All these years. All. These." She stops. "So many lies."

"I didn't mean to ..."

"The police will be coming. They'll ask you. You'll need to be clear about what you want to say."

"You're going to phone them?"

"I don't think I'll have to, do you?" She smiles sadly. She's aged since this morning—her skin is grey and creased, her eyes are swollen. "Oh, Finn." She crouches in front of him and holds his hands. Her fingers caress his gold wedding ring. "Even if you lie to everyone else ... I need to ..." Her voice cracks. She swallows and takes a breath. "I need to know."

"It was twenty years ago—"

"Don't. I remember the day you walked into the library. I remember the paper you read. I remember the first book I gave you to read. Do *not* tell me you don't remember."

CHAPTER TWENTY-SEVEN

LEXI

It's a dream; it has to be.

You're in bed on Midsummer's Day, anticipating the moment your alarm will break into the early morning tranquility. Finn's asleep beside you, nestled into his pillow, with the duvet barely covering his chest. And you're never drinking whatever you were on last night again.

Yet you're cold, in the middle of a heatwave—you've forgotten how it feels. Should you be shivering quite so ferociously? The dampness permeates your skin, deep down into your bones. The smell of sodden mud and rotting leaves hangs in the air.

And it's not a dream. The world is chaotic and intolerable—too much disorder after too much silence. The clamor attacks you and you cover your ears and hunker down to blunt the noise. Dogs bark at each other when they pass in the street; wind blows through the trees and their branches bend and creak; seagulls screech, catching you by surprise. People go about their business as if nothing extraordinary is occurring, and you want to stop each person and tell them that, yes, something very out of the ordinary is happening to you.

You're with Finn again, back where you belong. But he doesn't see you, of course. You fill with a love which has been missing for so long.

And how long it's been. Look at him: he's old. His hair is dirty grey and barely there on top; his eyes are puffy and tired, a little sunken into blemished skin. You want to reach out and trace the lines of his wrinkles, but you resist, afraid of him sensing you.

It's strange to see him like this. A moment ago, he was youthful and energized. Muscles rippled beneath his T-shirts, his eyes sparkled mischievously, and he attracted far too many smiles from other women. Now his movements are precise, as though he has to prepare for them in advance. The furrow between his eyebrows is deepened.

Focused on Finn, you haven't noticed the woman on the sofa, almost folded in on herself, so petite and pale. She's chewing on her thumbnail while staring at Finn as if she's asked a question and awaiting the reply. But it's not a reply he wants to give, because he's avoiding her eye.

You stand. Do you need to do that anymore, or is it a remnant of your previous corporeal existence?

On the mantelpiece is a photo in a silver frame—Finn and this woman wearing a wedding dress. He got married. You tremble slightly, catch yourself. It could have been you. Why wasn't it you?

He's not smiling in the picture. She's resting her head on his shoulder, a sleepy smile playing on her lips, eyes closed with contentment. Finn is far away and pensive, as if fearful of the future he's created for himself.

Back in the room, you try to focus on their conversation. Their mouths are moving, but the words are concealed by the tumult of other noises. You shut your eyes to concentrate. *Lexi. So many lies. The police.* Fragments of sentences seeping towards you.

Finn looks resolutely into the room, staring at nothing, his fingers drumming a nervous beat on the arm of the chair. He shakes his head a lot. He gives single word replies to her questions. The gruff monotone retort which is so familiar.

"Did you do it?" Amber's question. The only question which matters.

You want to run, to escape, to never hear Finn's answer. But you sit beside him again. The draught you create causes Finn's hair to waft.

Did you do it?

"Don't tell me you don't remember," his wife says through the constant barrage of sound, of a clock ticking and the buzz of appliances around the house.

She stifles a sob and rushes from the room. It's just you and Finn now. He turns slightly, catching your eye, if such a thing were possible. He smiles with an air of reminiscence, and you wonder if he can see you after all, if he always sees you—last thing at night when the sky is riddled with stars, and at the first hint of dawn, and in the long hours between.

"Lexi," he says. It's more of a sigh, your name escaping by accident.

"I'm here." You rest your hand over his, but you don't feel the tissue-paper skin or rough tracks of his veins.

He looks directly at you, and his expression changes to one of sorrow and yearning. "You look just how I remember." He chuckles to himself. "Of course you do. This wretched head can never forget you."

Did you do it?

It's your question too, but you don't need Finn's reply. You know. He killed you.

"I'm here. I'm not a memory. I'm holding your hand."

He doesn't hear you; he's having his own inaccessible conversation.

You should be yelling at this man who stole your life from you. You should be brimming with hate and vengeance, seething with anger and rage. Maybe you would have been, once, but you're exhausted. The lives you've led—the one before, and the one today—have been good lives. You've been content, for some of it. You've even been happy on occasion.

So instead, you want to ask him all the things you would if you happened upon him in the street one day, if you shyly asked if he wanted to grab a coffee and he accepted. You want to know how old his kids are and what they're called; if he made it to a Rugby World Cup final at some point; if *he* was happy and had a good life too.

You draw breath to clear your thoughts. Except you don't because you have no breath to take. No heartbeat. No blood pulsing through your veins. There hasn't been all day. For a long, long time.

Finn shifts in his seat and glances out of the window when Amber returns. She's dabbing her eyes with a tissue and drinking from a wine glass. She hasn't brought one for Finn. You smirk when he realizes he doesn't have a drink; you like her.

"I told people she'd left me," he says. "Went. That's the word I used. I didn't know how else to phrase it. *When Lexi went.*" He lets out an agonized moan. "I should have confessed, but I started to believe it." He looks at her, at you. "Tell me what to do."

"Tell the truth," you whisper. "You owe me that much."

CHAPTER TWENTY-EIGHT

FINN

Finn's face is ashen and desolate. His fingers scratch at the seam of his trousers. Amber is numb, waiting. The house is suddenly icy.

"I pushed her."

It was more than a push. He remembers a shove. His frustration and anger merging, bubbling over. He'd thought they were happy, content. A relationship which fitted together without the requirement to be worked on.

His mates' marriages looked so complicated. He always said Lexi was unique because she didn't need the things that their partners did. Happy to watch him play rugby and grab a takeaway on the way home, she didn't demand expensive weekend breaks to Paris or Venice, he told them, or surprise bouquets of flowers.

He wasn't a man to use the word *soulmate*, but if he thought about it long enough, that's what he meant. Lexi was the woman he'd grow old with. And here she was on the verge of leaving him, telling him it was all a lie. He couldn't go through another breakup. Claire left; Lexi couldn't.

She clung to him on the stairs, and he needed a moment to process it all. Just needed her to stop her infernal, drunken wailing. Needed to get out of his suit and into shorts because the evening was so clammy. Needed a second to himself. And she wouldn't stop.

She stumbled, lost her footing and grappled for his arm, but he raised it above his head petulantly so she couldn't reach. Such a childish, stupid thing to do, in her state. She fumbled for his shirt, but it was tight against his chest. Buttons popped. Cotton tore. When he brought his arm back down, it struck her.

Time stopped.

Lexi's hair floated around her, as though she was lying on the surface of a crystal-clear lake. A moment of perfection, an enigmatic smile on her lips.

CHAPTER TWENTY-NINE

LEXI

You didn't fall. You weren't pushed. You grabbed for him, to unsteady *him*, to force him back downstairs. To talk. Just that. When it didn't work, when you couldn't budge his heavy, muscular frame, you threw yourself backwards. You wanted to see the panic in Finn's eyes. Wanted him to be terrified of losing you.

It started with a giggle. A smirk as the idea flashed in front of you. How funny it would be if ...

He'd see his error and rush to catch you.

You hung in the air almost forever—arms and legs star-shaped. Nothing moved. Time froze. Finn gazed down at you like he did the day he met you. Captivated, enamored. And you wanted him more than ever. You wanted to climb back up the fractured air between you, clamber back through the seconds. Rewind time. Be safe in his embrace.

You saw the alarm and fear on his face. You heard your name, but it was so far away.

CHAPTER THIRTY

FINN

She fell so slowly, almost gracefully. There was a moment, after the smirk but before the confusion and realization, where she was divine and flawless. Held in the moment, caught between breaths.

The image is seared into his mind. She's there when he closes his eyes at night, when he opens them in the half-light of a winter's morning.

It seemed he had all the time in the world to reach out for her, but he couldn't move.

He called her name, and the sound stretched forever.

CHAPTER THIRTY-ONE

LEXI

You lay immobile on the floor, arms and legs tucked awkwardly beneath your crumpled, broken body. You thought it would hurt. You heard the sickeningly hollow thud of your head hitting the bottom step. You waited for the pain to sear through your skull.

But it never came.

You felt nothing at all. Nothing beneath you. Nothing above. The sun was too bright, dazzling you—an almost magical haze wrapping itself around you, like a cloud. Or a fog.

You were sleepy, drifting into a dream. Certain you'd feel better in the morning when you woke, when you shrugged off the hangover and apologized to Finn. Oh god, another apology. It seemed you were always saying sorry for one thing or another. You needed to change; you *would* change; you needed to stop repeating the same mistakes. It was time to grow up and decide what you really wanted. You only have one life, after all—you have to make it count.

"I'm sorry," you murmured, but the words melted on your lips.

And you forgot. You forgot the day and the week, and the year. And all the years before.

Faces passed in front of you. Vanessa and Cassie and Mila, your colleagues at work, and the people who caught the same bus as you morning after morning, Phoebe, and your parents. None of them remained. Enveloped by a mist, becoming ghosts, becoming fictions.

CHAPTER THIRTY-TWO

FINN

Sprawled on the tiled floor, a small wound bleeding on the side of her head, Lexi could have been sleeping. Her expression as composed and enchanting as the moment before she woke on a Saturday morning, the only day when Finn had a chance of waking before her.

Her stillness was unsettling. Finn sat on the second to top step, immobilized by the shock. Heart pounding violently. He thought he was rushing towards her, cradling her head, calling for help.

But he wasn't.

He shuffled to the next step down.

A red puddle seeped across the floor. A moan or a sigh, that's all he needed to hear from her to break this spell of paralysis. Another step down. His stomach knotted in terror. Just a flicker, or a twitch. Something. Please.

On the penultimate step, Finn's heels were tucked against the riser, knees pressed into his chest. Unwilling to put a foot on the floor where she lay. A tiny bunched-up ball of a man.

"Lexi?" His voice lost in the silence.

He bent forward and hesitated before taking her hand. His thumb stroked her wrist. She always giggled and tried to pull away when he did that; it was the most ticklish part of her. He always followed it with a kiss, pulling her close and leaving her weak.

Her skin was warm, but already waxy and pale. No pulse.

He needed to get help, but his legs faltered as he tried to stand. Bile rose to his throat.

"Oh, shit. Oh, shit."

In a trance, he fumbled for his phone, his hand hovering over the screen, finger poised on the 9. The moment looped around his head. The push, the fall, the stomach-wrenching thump when she reached the bottom.

He'd done this.

He'd pushed her.

Killed her.

It was an accident. He couldn't catch her. He hadn't meant to let her fall.

But the neighbors must have seen them arrive home, had almost certainly heard the fight. Curtains twitching as people peered through them, gathering titbits to pass on to anyone who asked. Someone might have already called the police. He looked like a menacing sort, they'd told Lexi once, before they knew she and him were together.

What happened, sir? The paramedics would have to ask. The police too. And he wouldn't be able to tell them. He'd stare vacantly and shake his head because anything else would be a confession, he'd incriminate himself. His life ruined over one stupid mistake.

But wasn't it what he *should* do, what any normal person *would* do?

He stared at Lexi, but it wasn't her anymore—just the vessel she once was.

Could he run away? How far could he get in one night? Far enough.

They'd find the body, of course, in a few days' time. Those busybodies next door would call round, on account of hearing suspicious noises, and be concerned there was no answer. Or Vanessa would start nosing around, peering through windows. Possibly Lexi's given her a key, for emergencies. She'd assume it was something to do with Finn. It could only be him, after all. The search would commence; he'd be a fugitive.

How far could he get in one night? Not far enough.

Finn squeezed past Lexi, careful not to disturb her, and in the kitchen poured himself a large whiskey, gulping it down like medicine. He cradled the glass and leant against the sink, gazing out into the garden. A black cat stretched lazily across the lawn. Sunset crested the rooftops, silhouetting the hedge.

Finn's fingers brushed the packets of seeds Lexi had bought a few days before, left there while she unpacked the rest of the shopping. Vegetable seeds, no flowers—she wanted to grow her own food and reduce unnecessary plastic. He poured himself another drink and took it back to Lexi at the bottom of the stairs.

"We were supposed to be together forever. I knew it the day I met you." A tear fell. "This is a mistake. You have to wake up, Lexi, you have to." He took a swig of whiskey and bent to hold her hand. "What am I going to do?"

The halo of blood had stopped spreading. Finn watched the edges congeal.

He paced. When he could no longer bear to look at her. Quick, abrupt strides along the hall—five, six of them—pivoting and returning. Each time hoping she wouldn't be there anymore and the need to decide would be redundant; that in the brief moment he wasn't looking she'd manage to crawl out of the house. He pictured her dragging herself along the road. *He tried to kill me*, she'd cry to the first passing stranger. He'd have to stop her, of course.

"I can't let you leave, can I?" Crouched beside her, stroking her cheek. "You have to stay here with me. I'm not a murderer."

The words rattled around the house.

"Shit, Lexi. What have I done?"

It grew dark around them on Lexi's last night. Finn's thoughts were wild and unsettled as he tried to make sense of the day.

And eventually there were no more back and forths, no more ifs or buts or maybes. The tiny seed of an idea matured; the need to make the problem disappear, to make Lexi disappear. People might not consider her absence odd, in fairness. She was going to leave him, anyway, one day—the neighbors will have noticed the tension and arguments, the slammed doors and his late-night drives just to get away from her. She'll have bored her friends with tales of woe. Who wouldn't notice when bright, bubbly Lexi—who never deserved to be tied down, who wasn't meant for an ordinary man like him—was suffering?

He knelt beside her and kissed her forehead and went outside to dig a hole.

Dawn broke in a ray of purple as Finn patted down the vegetable patch, dampening the soil with tears; Lexi's sheet-wrapped body several feet below.

On the longest day of the year, with the sun not quite risen, her alarm wouldn't go off for another hour and a half. Finn reluctantly left Lexi alone and went to bed. He closed his eyes and succumbed to a deep, exhausted abyss.

CHAPTER THIRTY-THREE

LEXI

Your skin is translucent, like an old woman's. Your fingers curl arthritically, your nails are brittle; veins protrude. Wrinkles appear. Your eyes sink into deep, discolored hollows.

Weariness falls upon you. Not the insomnia you've existed on so far, but overwhelming fatigue. All the days and months and years you never lived.

"I didn't realize anyone was watching," Finn says. He shakes his head and allows tears to fall down his face without wiping them away. "She was just a child ... Oh, that poor woman." He imagines Georgie or Isla at the age of four trying to make sense of something like that. "All these years, she knew what I'd done. I almost ..."

The confession doesn't bring him the relief he hoped it might. His guilt obscured for so long rises quickly, scratching into every cell of his body like a disease ripping him apart. He dabs his tears away with a handkerchief from his pocket. He never used to carry one. Is there an age when men feel the time is right to have one? A celebration of longevity, marked with a square of fabric.

"I still don't understand how you could have done it," Amber says. She's sitting as far away from him as possible. "Hidden her away all this time. Lied to her friends and family. Tell me it isn't true. Tell me there's been a terrible mistake."

He looks at you with dull, remorseful eyes. "I would have told someone. Before I died, I would have told them where you were. Where *she* was." He looks at Amber. "I would have told someone."

Poor Amber, who smiles softly but cannot hold his gaze, who waits with Finn but cannot bring herself to offer comfort. He's not the man either of you thought he was. Her marriage has been a lie. And her poor children! How can she begin to explain?

Finn leans back, allowing his body to sink into the chair, letting his head rest against the cushion. "I'm sorry. I'm so sorry." He emits intermittent sobs.

While Amber apparently retains her indifference, the sound slices into you. Because you love him, this man who cut short your life. You love him because he's the only person you've ever loved. And it doesn't change. No matter how far away you are, deep down part of you is always in love. You want to hold him and stop him hurting. You want to shield him from what's coming next.

"I know," you reply. But your voice doesn't exist anymore.

His wife stands at the window, gazing into the street and across the opposite rooftops to the river beyond, these last few minutes of calm before everything changes. The years spent enjoying this view are tainted.

"What should I tell Georgie and Isla?" It's not a question for Finn, or for anyone. Her first instinct as a mother is to protect her kids, but how can she? Everyone will know soon enough:

her friends, their friends, their friends' parents, the teachers at school, her colleagues at the library. An endless list of people who'll be pointing and gossiping. She can't lie to them—it's too late for lies.

The doorbell rings. You all turn and stare into the hall. It's as silent as anything you have heard all day.

Amber answers and two police officers enter the house. Finn rises from the chair, bones creaking, with a small involuntary grunt. He reaches for Amber's hand, and this time she's there for him. Because she loves him too and it won't ever change. The father of her children, her true love.

One of the PCs reads Finn his rights. "You understand what's happening, sir?"

He nods. "Are you going to put handcuffs on me? My wrists are rather sore."

"No, I don't think we need to do that."

The other takes his arm, though, and escorts him from the house. Neighbors are gathered in tight clusters along the curb or leaning on their garden walls, respectfully, solemnly.

You don't follow. You stand with Amber and watch Finn— so scared and frail—fold into the back seat of the police car. It takes an age to pull away. And when it does, he's staring straight ahead. The neighbors peel away. One or two nod their acknowledgement of Amber, but she doesn't respond. You remain there long after there's anything to see, the two of you together.

Outside, the smooth, glassy river you've spent eternity gazing at is choppy and churning into white peaks. There's no sun— heavy grey clouds obscure it. You're mesmerized by its swirling and swishing.

Amber's anger and confusion are raw and embedded, while yours have been cast aside, stacked up all around town in piles of stones. You're drained of the pain, ready to move on.

Maybe if you stood closer, she'd sense you and you'd be able to comfort her, let some of your release be transferred to her. Maybe.

You rest your hand on her shoulder as she hunches over with waves of crying convulsing her body. For a second, you feel her spry bony arms through the sleeve of her cardigan, the sweet perfume dabbed beneath her jaw fills the air. And possibly, she looks at you and opens her mouth in astonishment, and holds her hand to your face, the one which no longer exists. You smile; you hope she sees it. But the room is starting to lose coherence. It's starting to fade.

And the weight of your years vanishes; the fatigue disperses.

And you're aware of people you haven't seen for so long emerging beside you.

And your parents are in front of you, as if they've never been anywhere else, and they open their arms to you.

And you're safe again. In your movement, there's a lightness you can hardly control.

And you're ready to go, because it's time.

And.

ACKNOWLEDGEMENTS

Thank you to the publishing dream-team, Jessica Bell and Amie McCracken, and to Elaina Battista-Parsons, who advocated for this novel's acceptance. And to Melanie Faith, my editor once again.

None of it would have been possible without the advice, encouragement, and nudges in the right direction from my beta readers: Martha Engber, Nick Wilford, and Ruth Schiffman.

There are small areas in the novel which needed a bit of research into the police side of things, so I'm very grateful to PS B Harrild-Pine for answering some probably very silly questions.

I also need to mention ... —oh no, am I really going to go there? Yep!

This novel was written/rewritten during COVID, when we had a full house again, furniture had to be moved to accommodate us all, and my desk ended up in a bay window which captured the searing heatwave sun until late afternoon. As part of this novel is set in a heatwave, the experience was very useful, if a little uncomfortable.

My town stepped up to the lockdown regulations in the most amazing manner, and during my daily walks with my canine muse, I came to really understand the crushing oppression of the heat and silence which Lexi endures. I'd written a lot of the novel before 2020 but experiencing the empty streets caused me to rewrite a lot of it.

So, thank you COVID, I guess?

And finally, huge and continual thanks to my husband Peter, my sons Connor and Ollie, the muse Artoo, and all my friends and family who give me a shoulder to bang my head against and are willing to listen to my monologues as I try to work out the latest plot issue. You're the best!

VINE LEAVES PRESS

Enjoyed this book?
Go to *vineleavespress.com* to find more.
Subscribe to our newsletter: